F Amo

Amor, Paul Fusey, 1943-

The People's Republic

FORT MYERS - LEE COUNTY LIBRARY
Lee County Library System
2050 Lee Street
Fort Myers, Florida 33901
"Books may be returned to any
library in the system."

THE
PEOPLE'S
REPUBLIC

THE PEOPLE'S REPUBLIC

A Novel

Paul Fusey Amor

WALKER AND COMPANY
New York

Copyright © 1989 by Paul Fusey Amor

All rights reserved. No part of this book may be reproduced or transmitted in any form or by any means, electronic or mechanical, including photocopying, recording, or by any information storage and retrieval system, without permission in writing from the Publisher.

All the characters and events portrayed in this story are fictitious.

First published in the United States of America in 1989 by Walker Publishing Company, Inc.

Published simultaneously in Canada by Thomas Allen & Son Canada, Limited, Markham, Ontario.

Library of Congress Cataloging-in-Publication Data

Amor, Paul Fusey, 1943–
The People's Republic : a novel / Paul Fusey Amor.
    p. cm.
ISBN 0-8027-1072-7
1. China—History—1949–1976—Fiction. I. Title.
PS3551.M575P46 1989
813'.54—dc20   89-9037
CIP

Printed in the United States of America

10 8 6 4 2 1 3 5 7 9

To Min Jin

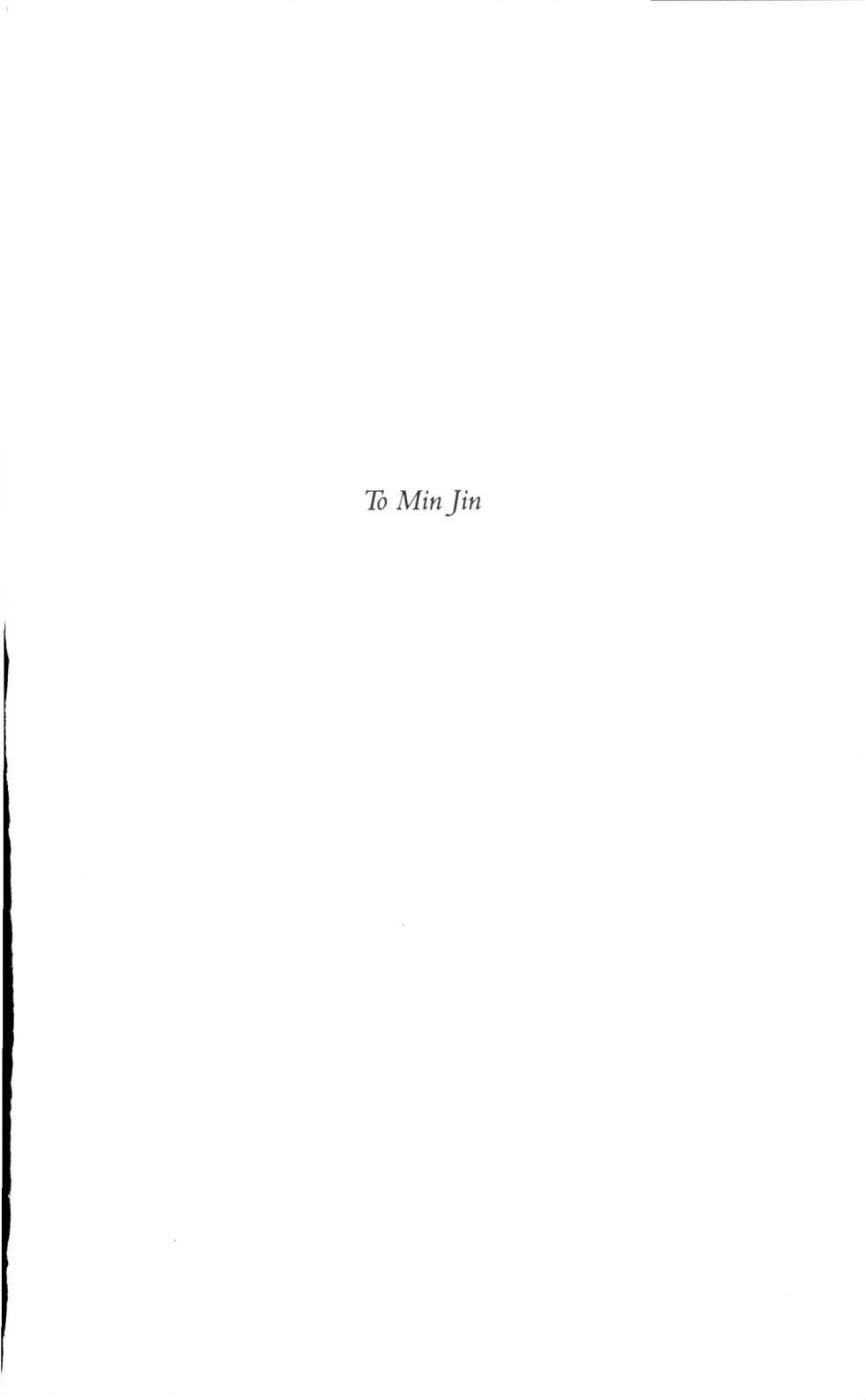

"In all things there are contradictions."

—Mao Tse-Tung

THE
PEOPLE'S
REPUBLIC

CHAPTER ONE

China: 1960

THE air felt strange that first night when we put down in Shanghai. It was damp, and a mist hid the plane while we waited in the terminal for the refueling to finish. It was my first time in China, and everything was exciting, the way it always is when you come to a new country. But this wasn't Spain or Italy. This was enemy territory—I could not afford a single mistake.

My instructions were simple: "There is a man in Turpan. He has information that has been paid for. You will proceed to Turpan, where he will contact you." What that information was I wasn't told. They are clever that way; they protect themselves as much as possible. By "themselves" I mean the organization. It has rules, you see, commandments of a sort, and the first one is "Thou shalt protect the Agency."

If you studied a map of China you would find Turpan in the far northwest corner, in the center of a province called Xinjiang. It's a godforsaken place full of rock and sand, burning hot in the summer and freezing cold in the winter. The people are mostly Moslems, Uighurs who look more like Turks than Chinese. Close by are the Pamir Mountains, where Afghanistan, Russia, Pakistan, and

China meet in a crazy region of great mountains and rocky, bone-dry plateaus. The people here don't take well to outside rule—they fight because for them freedom is more important than life itself.

I had no such illusions about what I was doing and why. I've never believed in holy causes, perhaps because there's a lot of dirty work in my line of business. Whenever it got to me I always told myself, "You can retire in twenty years and move to Mexico and forget all about it. Sure, you'll have trouble sleeping some nights, but the feelings will pass. People learn to live with things—that's what life is about." I thought I was hardened—not tough, just hard, with a hide like a crocodile.

I had been with the Agency close to twenty years and was a realist about my future. I was someone waiting to retire and slide out of view, good for a pick-up or a drop-off—a courier. They wouldn't use me for anything bigger. In my file, I was sure, there was a letter that said, "Not entirely politically reliable."

I guess somewhere along the line one of the bright boys from Yale or Princeton had decided I wasn't exactly hardcore. "This man's commitment is lukewarm—he won't go the last mile."

They flew me into China with a Canadian passport that said I was Jake Siever, businessman, from Windsor, Ontario. I stayed in Beijing for a week, playing the game of being a tourist. Chinese security was probably watching me, but their agents were hard to spot. They might be sitting at the table next to yours in a restaurant, or maybe the attendant who cleaned your room and made your bed was one. It didn't matter. Later, when I went west, I knew I would be able to pick them out. If the same man follows you in two towns, you have him pegged.

The flight to Urumchi where I would make connections for Turpan took three hours. The seats were small and crammed together, three on each side of the aisle in an old plane that was designed for half as many passengers as it was carrying. From the window everything was brown or gray except for the snow-covered tops of a chain of mountains. I could make out a railway line, a lone thread in a great desert. We flew over the last range of snow-capped mountains and began to descend through clouds. Beneath, Urumchi loomed up, a welter of buildings beneath a blanket of smog.

I had arranged for two representatives of the travel service to meet me at the airport because I thought I'd better continue playing the tourist.

The guide was a fat man in a blue Mao coat and cap with a big smile, all teeth, but when you looked at his eyes you read something else. There was a woman with him, small and shy. She was the translator, but her English was barely intelligible.

The trip to my hotel took about an hour. Over everything hung a thick layer of smoke that obscured the sun and turned the snow beside the roadway gray. Now and then we passed Uighurs. They ignored us and stared ahead as they bounced along in their ass-drawn carts.

We cut through the center of town, a collection of shacks with mud walls and a few large Soviet-style buildings, then began a climb up a long, poplar-lined avenue. On one side of the road was the Uighur ghetto, and I could see old men dressed in black corduroy and fur-trimmed hats walking slowly with canes and a myriad of dirty, ragged children. The road climbed until it left the city behind, went over the top of a ridge, then down into a valley. We turned off the road and came to an open space in the middle of a forest of pine, passed a gate guarded by soldiers who looked young and unmilitary with their tan canvas shoes, then came out into an open area. Beyond were the mountains, their peaks glittering in the sunlight, and at the back of the open space were two modern-looking buildings with large windows facing the mountains. The car drove up to one of these. An attendant carried my bags in, and they showed me to a large room filled with sunlight.

The translator mumbled something that I gathered meant I should rest and that dinner would be ready in two hours, then I was left alone. I stretched out on the bed and stared at the ceiling, trying to collect my thoughts. Obviously the best thing to do was wait. I would have to establish an itinerary that looked regular to them—so regular that they would get a little sloppy; then I would make my move. There was no sense in trying anything for a while, though. They had put me in a hotel so far from the center of town that there was no way I could make a move without their knowing it. I opened my suitcase, took out the bottle of brandy I had brought with me, and poured myself half a glass. I needed something to help bide my time, and the brandy would do as well as anything else. It didn't taste bad and it took the edge off the world so that, for a while anyway, the claws and teeth of the monsters waiting out there didn't seem so terrifying.

The food in the hotel was bad. There was coffee and bread and butter and an assortment of dishes, each tasting a little worse than the other. I contented myself with the bread and butter and asked for a second pot of coffee. Finally, I climbed the stairs to my room, undressed, and lay in my bed. Eventually I got around to the bottle of Chinese brandy again. After three glasses the world looked a little better, and I opened the curtains and stared out.

The peaks of the mountains in the distance glittered like alabaster. There was something cold and austere yet pure about them, and I felt good just looking at them. I must have fallen asleep, for the next thing I knew, the sun was shining and I could hear the voices of the maids in the hallway outside my room. My head was clear and I felt rested and good. Everything was perfect except for one small detail. Before going to dinner I had laid my passport on the desk so that it was at a forty-five degree angle to the left edge. It was still on the desk, but now it was perpendicular to the edge. A maid might have moved it, but it was unlikely that a maid would have worked during the night.

Chapter Two

On the second afternoon I let the guide take me to a store where native products were sold. I bought a rug, a purple skullcap, and two bracelets of pale green jade, though God knew who I would give them to. We returned to the hotel late in the afternoon, and I told the guide that I would not need him or the translator the following day and would have the hotel phone the travel service if I wanted them again. I expected an argument, but they said nothing, and a little later I watched them climb into their car and drive away. That night I told the people at the hotel to arrange for a railroad ticket to Xi'an, a large town about five hundred miles to the east. The stop for Turpan lay on the same line, a hundred miles due east of Urumchi.

On the train there was one car of closed compartments, and I seemed to be the only one on it. I had brought two suitcases, and I put these above the seat opposite me and watched the scenery pass. The train chugged through a narrow pass. Beyond, the terrain turned flat, mostly desert—pebbles and brown rock dotted here and there with shrubs. Soon the monotony of it put me to sleep.

I was awakened by a rap on the door and pushed it open

to see a blue-suited female attendant accompanied by another woman in a dirty white jacket and dirtier apron. The attendant wore pigtails and had a chubby peasant's face. She stood with her hands thrust into the pockets of her trousers like a girl scout, and by gestures asked if I wanted to eat. I nodded.

Half an hour later there was another rap. The woman in white had returned with a tray containing dishes of rice and soup, fried pork, celery, and onions. It was the first decent food I'd had in days. I gobbled it like a starving man, drank some tea, and resumed watching the desert roll past. It was seven thirty P.M. and the sun still hung high over the horizon. I realized with a sinking feeling that it would not be dark at nine when we reached Turpan. We were on Beijing time but we were far to the west. I had been a fool not to have remembered that, because it would make carrying out my plan more difficult.

I took the suitcases down and opened one, removed the rug I had bought and rolled it into a shape like a man, and covered it with a blanket I found in the compartment. In the darkness it would look like a sleeping man. Then I opened the other suitcase and took out the blue pants and jacket I had brought from Beijing, changed into these, and exchanged my shoes for black corduroy sneakers. Next I opened a case and took out a stick of yellow-brown paste and rubbed it in my hands until it was soft, then smeared the cream onto my face, inspecting the results in the mirror. In the half light of the car my skin looked almost yellow. Finally I opened a small tin that contained lampblack and rubbed it into my hair. The result would fool no one in the clear light of day, but at dusk it would do the trick.

I checked my watch—eight forty-five—and pushed the

curtain to the side and stared out. The train was passing through the desert, but I could tell from the sound of the wheels and from the speed we were going that we were descending into the basin where Turpan lay. Then the wheels began to scream against the metal of the tracks as the engineer braked the train, and my heart began to race.

The dishes from dinner still sat on the small table before the window. That would give them an excuse to open the door and check on me, so I put them on the tray, cautiously opened the door of the compartment, and set it outside.

The train clicked over some switches as we passed the control tower at the entrance of the station. A voice in the speaker under the window said that we were entering Turpan. Then, with a lurch, we stopped. I grabbed one suitcase, slid the compartment door open, stepped out, and slid it shut again, then walked briskly toward the far end of the car. I was almost at the end when a conductor passed. He looked at me curiously, but I kept walking; when he called after me I did not turn back.

Chapter Three

The station was crowded and the platform filled with milling people, all rushing to find a seat on the train. I pushed through the crowd and joined the line at the exit. People had to show their tickets as they left, to prove they had ridden legally, and I expected a problem because my ticket said Xi'an. The woman looked at it, then pointed toward the station, and when I tried to push past her, she stopped me and pointed to the station again: she wanted me to go to the agent and get a refund for the unused part of the ticket. There was no point in arguing, and the longer I waited the more attention I would draw, so I turned and walked toward the station.

I had just begun to push the door open when I saw the conductor again standing in the middle of the room, talking to two white-coated policemen. Quickly I moved back into the shadows on the platform. There were only a few people still there, some waving to the people already on the train, others pushing carts that contained apples and bags of peanuts. Through the window of the station I could see the conductor and the policemen talking; then they turned and started toward the door. I pressed myself into the shadows beside a large column and watched them walk to the train and the conductor step aboard just before it started to move again.

I glanced toward the exit gate. The ticket collector had gone and the gate was shut, but it might not be locked. I took a half-dozen steps, gripped the handle, and tried to push it open. It did not move, and I broke out in a cold sweat. I could see the policemen still standing on the platform. One of them had lit a cigarette. I tried the gate again, then saw a latch and lifted it. The gate rolled open smoothly, and I stepped through and vanished into the shadows of the buildings that lined the street leading to the station.

The moon was full, and the bright moonlight cast distinct shadows. The buildings were dark and the air freezing. I shivered and realized that I was soaked through with perspiration. According to the briefing the Agency had given me, the bus depot lay at the end of the road. From the depot it was over fifty miles to the oasis of Turpan. Between lay desert.

I came on the station suddenly. There was a high wall around it, and a large gate in this led to a courtyard. The front door of the station building was open, and inside several people were huddled around a stove, sleeping. I moved to a far corner and squatted with my back against the wall. It was nine twenty P.M. and the bus would not leave until eight A.M. I shut my eyes and tried to sleep. Somewhere beyond—somewhere across fifty miles of rock and gravel—the contact was waiting. "There is a man in Turpan" was all I had been told. Once I had arrived he would find me. It seemed like a fairytale, some strange story out of the Arabian Nights. I shifted my weight so that it was supported by the wall, and yielded to sleep.

The shuffle of feet and the groan of people stretching sleep-stiffened limbs woke me. The people huddled around the stove were stirring. A small window at the far end of the station now had a light behind it. Then it opened and men began buying tickets.

Two men pushed in front of me and began arguing with the ticket seller. I looked at the clock on the wall. It said seven forty-five. The argument grew louder. I watched the minute hand on the clock move. It was now seven fifty and there was no indication that the argument would end.

The men who had pushed in front of me had Arabic features. One was heavyset; he did the arguing. The other, with a livid white scar from the corner of his eye almost to his chin, said nothing. It was now seven fifty-five. I shouldered the stocky man aside, put down a ten-yuan bill, and said "Turpan." The clerk took the bill, but before he could give me the ticket, the stocky man had pushed back in front of me and begun arguing again. I put my hand on his shoulder and thrust him aside and claimed the place by the window. In a second he was back, yelling at me this time. I ignored him, concentrating on the clerk, who gave me a ticket and some bills for change.

At the end of a row of buses, one was revving its motor. I made for this and stepped aboard, tugging my suitcase after me. The bus was packed, three and sometimes four people crammed into each seat where there was space for only two. People jammed the aisle. Small children were crying.

The driver ground the gears, and with a lurch the bus moved forward, turned, and went through the gate at the front of the station. It rumbled down the street that led to the train station, then turned left onto a paved road that led out into the desert. Here the bus picked up speed, bouncing over the bumps and craters that dotted the roadway.

Soon I became drowsy, but each time I began to fall asleep I was jolted awake by a new bump. Across the aisle, a child began to cry, then vomited, and its mother held it in front of her until it was finished, then lifted it back to her shoulder. The smell of the vomit mingled with that of sweat, garlic, unwashed bodies, and exhaust fumes from the engine.

After two hours the desert gave way to thickets of poplars. A building appeared, then another, and soon we were passing clusters of flat-roofed buildings made of mud. We passed a commune gate, a large red star over it. There were more buildings and suddenly we were in the center of town, weaving through narrow twisting streets that led to an open field behind ramshackle buildings. Here the bus stopped and the passengers got out.

I pushed my way off and followed the crowd toward a square in the center of town lined with booths and crates, where Uighurs were selling meat and bread and clothes. On one side of the square a number of small shops were built against a great wall. One of these was a restaurant, and I went in.

Two Uighurs sitting at a table looked up as I entered, and followed me with hard, cold eyes. A Chinese dressed in black with a white skullcap and a greasy apron was standing at the back of the restaurant. Before him were plates of boiled mutton, skewers of shish kebab, and stacks of flat bread. I pointed to the shish kebab and held up two fingers, then at the bread. He handed me the food and I gave him a five-yuan note. He made change, counting it slowly and studying me as he handed it back. There was a puzzled expression on his face.

The shish kebab was juicy and had a good, smoky taste. Then I ate the bread, saving half a piece, which I jammed into the pocket of my coat. As I left I felt the eyes of the men follow me.

I was tired and wanted to rest, but was afraid to stop and wandered around the square. As long as I kept moving, mingling with the crowd, no one would look too closely at me. When night came I could find a place to sleep and rub some of the yellow paste on my face.

The suitcase had begun to feel like a heavy weight, and my shoulder ached. I decided to return to the bus station and check it in in the baggage room until evening, so I began to walk back up the alleyway that led to the main street. I had almost reached the end when a voice somewhere behind me said, in Chinese, "Take the second street past the station and go into the shop that sells glass."

Chapter Four

The street was narrow and angled off the main street at about forty-five degrees. I moved slowly, peering closely at each building I passed. First were some shops, but none of these sold glass, then a blacksmith, then the front walls of the courtyards of houses, their gates closed. I walked for about half a mile, then stopped. Had I been mistaken? Was this really the second street?

I had begun to retrace my steps when I became aware that someone was walking close behind me. I stopped and waited, and an old man, dressed in black, hobbled past.

I speeded up and had almost reached the main street again when I passed a woman who was baking flat bread in an oven. The bread was stacked on a table beside the oven, and I took two pieces and paid her.

I watched her work while I ate. Again I thought of the voice. It had not been my imagination. Perhaps I had taken the wrong turn, or perhaps I had not walked far enough down the street. I would try again.

When I finished the bread I hoisted my suitcase and started toward the main street again. I had a strange sensation and was suddenly aware that the woman baking the bread was watching me. Then she seemed to look to the side, to somewhere behind me, almost leading my eyes in that direction.

I followed her gaze and saw the front of a house with two windows. Half the spaces in the windows were filled with waxed paper instead of glass. Between these two windows was a door, and above it a small, hand-painted picture of plates and cups. Because I had been looking for a shop that sold panes of glass, I had passed by without noticing the sign.

I went to the door and knocked, a voice muttered within, and I pushed the door open and entered. The room was in semi-darkness, and at first I saw no one and stood, suitcase in hand, staring into that darkness.

"Shut the door!" said a voice. When I turned around, my eyes had adjusted to the light, and I could see a slim man standing beside a curtained entrance to an inner room. He was studying me coolly. Finally he motioned me forward, stepped to the front door and placed a bar across it, then pointed to the curtained opening that led to the other room.

Here a lone lightbulb hanging from the ceiling cast a weak, harsh light, and I could see him more clearly. He was a Chinese of indistinguishable age—he might have been anywhere from thirty-five to fifty. His cheekbones were high and his deep-set eyes glittered like coals.

"So you have come to buy some Uighur plates," he said in Mandarin. "I have many different kinds of plates. Some are clay, some are porcelain, some made in Turpan, and some in Kashgar."

"It is the plates made in Turpan that I seek," I said.

"Such plates are very expensive," he said.

"The plates I seek have already been paid for," I answered. "I have come from Beijing to pick them up."

His eyes glittered but he made no move.

"I cannot wait long," I said. "Those who are following me will find me. I must have the plates before tonight or it will be too late."

When I said this the man smiled slyly, showing a set of stained teeth.

There was a rap on the door of the outer room, and we both turned. Neither made a move. Again a rap, and this time I could hear someone calling out in a gruff voice. The man lifted his hand and placed a finger before his mouth. For the first time his face had an expression—he seemed to be imploring me, almost begging that I say nothing to give us away.

We waited. Carts passed on the street outside, whips cracked, drivers clucked and urged their horses to move faster. Then there was another knock, again words from a gruff voice—this time they seemed louder—then the sound of someone pushing against the door, trying to force it open.

I looked at the shopkeeper. In place of the calm, expressionless mask that he had worn when he spoke to me was a look of terror. Then came a curse and the sound of footsteps as the knocker walked away.

The shopkeeper released his breath. His hands were shaking. I had the advantage and pressed it.

"You wait while the police come closer," I said.

Calm seemed to return to the man. Again he regarded me coolly.

"The plates were very expensive," he said. "The risk is great—I can make but one or two more purchases. I must have more money."

I turned and walked to the outer room, unbolted the door, and walked out into the street. To the man behind, waiting in the darkened shop, it might have seemed that I had acted impulsively. I had not—I had simply been following procedure. "If the source tries to alter the agreement in any way after payment has been made, the operative is to break off contact." Those were the words in the manual. I had done what I should so they could not fault me, and yet the material that I was to carry was not in my possession—if stopped I would be safe. I merely had to change back into my western clothes and resume the manner of a tourist.

I had walked almost a hundred yards down the main street, heading back toward the center of town, when I became aware that a man was following me. I did not need to turn and look to know who it was, and when I paused before a stand selling fruit I felt, pressed between the arm holding the suitcase and my side, a flat package wrapped in paper. I made a show of inspecting then rejecting a worm-eaten apple, then continued up the road, unobtrusively shifting the package to my free hand.

After a block I stopped to rest. The road was jammed with pedestrians and carts, and the going was slow. Suddenly I realized that I was very tired. I needed a place to rest—a bed and sleep. There was a hotel for foreigners, but I could not go there dressed as I was.

I crossed the street, dodging the moving asscarts, and bought two handfuls of peanuts from an old man. When he gave me my change I remained before his cart, cracking the nuts and watching the people pass. Then I bought another handful, and when he made my change I said, "Bingwan?"

He nodded in the direction I was going, and I stuffed the nuts into my pocket, lifted the suitcase, and trudged on. The parcel in my free hand was light, but somehow it seemed to me, just then, far heavier than the suitcase, and I found myself half wishing that the shopkeeper had stuck to his guns.

Chapter Five

The doorway of the hotel was covered with a dirty red blanket and there was no glass in the windows. I pushed the blanket aside and stepped into a darkened hallway. An old man hobbled toward me and said something in Uighur that I could not understand.

I took a five-yuan note from my pocket and handed it to him. Even in the darkened hallway I could see his greedy smile. He put the bill into his pocket and gave me four yuan, then took a key from a pegboard and led me up the hallway to an open courtyard paved with red tile. Doorways covered with red blankets surrounded the courtyard, and the old man hobbled to one of these, pushed back the blanket, and beckoned to me.

The room was small and dark; in one corner was a platform of bricks covered with a straw mat. A lightbulb dangled from the ceiling, and a stove made of bricks with a flue leading to a hole in the wall was built into the wall opposite the sleeping platform. A pile of coal lay on the floor before the stove.

The old man left, then reappeared with a shovel containing some glowing coals. He put these in the stove, then bowed and left.

I rummaged through my suitcase until I found the stick of yellow paste and began rubbing it on my face. I was dead tired and my eyes kept closing, but I forced myself to finish. I had no mirror to inspect the results, but I had used all the paste, so I had to be content. Then I chucked some more coal into the stove, shook out a blanket that lay at the foot of the platform, and lay down and covered myself. In a moment I fell into a deep sleep.

When I woke the room was ice cold and the blanket covering the doorway was flapping in the wind. I put on two sweaters under the blue jacket, dug through my suitcase and found the bottoms of a pair of long underwear, and hurriedly pulled these on. Still I was shivering. My western coat would have kept me warm, but I couldn't wear it while I was still masquerading.

Outside it was still light even though it was eight thirty. When I passed through the hallway to the street beyond, I met no one. I carried the parcel and my money and passport with me.

A block from the hotel I saw a lighted building with men inside seated at tables eating, and I entered. The restaurant served a thick soup with slices of omelette and pieces of mutton and onion in it. I bought a large bowl of this, two skewers of mutton and some bread, and took a seat at a long table where a half-dozen Uighurs were eating. Once I had drunk the soup and eaten the mutton I stopped shivering, and when I had finished the bread I felt full.

When I left the restaurant, darkness had fallen. Music from loudspeakers located atop a pole on every corner filled the air. The music was Arabic, a mournful, unending chant that rose and fell. The street was unlit, but here and there people had set up carts to sell fruit and nuts, and each of these had a small lantern hanging on it. I wanted to find the bus depot and learn when the next bus to the train station would leave, but I could not remember where it was.

For nearly an hour I wandered up and down the street, looking for the passageway that led to the depot. I had almost given up and was about to return to my hotel when I came to a place where the street widened and turned into a small square filled with carts and men roasting shish kebab and selling tea and bread.

Some men were squatting in a circle nearby. One of them must have made a joke, for suddenly there was an explosion of laughter. That was when I noticed the policeman staring at me.

My heart began to race, but I pretended I had not seen him. Sweat ran down my arms—I could feel the dampness in my palms. Suddenly the way out came—two Uighurs began to argue. One man pushed the other, and a crowd formed around them.

I was fifty yards down the street, walking as quickly as I could without attracting attention, when I heard a shout behind me. There was a side street ten yards ahead, and I made a dash for it. I sprinted wildly, not knowing where the street would lead or whether it would end in a cul-de-sac. I could hear someone behind me, grunting as he ran.

Suddenly I was confronted with a wall thirty feet high. There was no exit. I crouched in the darkness, waiting for the policeman.

Then I heard a soft whistle that seemed to come from somewhere behind the wall. There was a faint sound behind a gate in the wall—the moonlight reflected on it and I could see it move a few inches.

I moved to the gate and pushed against it. It yielded and

I slid through into a courtyard. The gate shut behind me, and I heard someone drop a bar in place.

Footsteps sounded outside; then they stopped. I held my breath. A minute passed; then the footsteps began again, sounding fainter and fainter. I breathed a sigh of relief, but before I could turn, the feel of cold steel against my skin froze me. Someone was holding a knife at my throat.

Chapter Six

I could hear them breathing in the darkness. They were listening, waiting to see what I would do.

There were whispers in the darkness. A light was turned on, and I found myself sitting in the midst of a half-dozen people. The oldest was a man about fifty, gray and grizzled, with a hook nose and fierce black eyes that glared at me from under bushy eyebrows. Two other men, one about thirty, the other a little younger, I assumed to be his sons—they both had his nose and eyes. The older woman was worn and thin, the other strikingly beautiful, with large eyes fringed with thick lashes. From behind the younger woman a boy of about five or six stared at me.

The younger son held the knife, but suddenly he smiled and tossed it onto a table on the other side of the room.

"Han policeman no good," he said in pidgin Chinese. "Han policeman afraid to come into Uighur house."

The men laughed and I joined them.

"You no Han," said the old man, staring hard at my face.

The older son reached over and rubbed my cheek, then pulled his hand away and inspected the yellow coloring on it. A sly expression crossed his face. "Russian," he said, and nodded knowingly to his brother.

I thought of letting him keep the idea, but then it occurred to me that Russians might be no more popular than Han. So I said, "American" and watched their faces.

The old man looked at me as if I had said I came from Mars.

"American!" repeated the younger son. He stood, muttering the word, then went to another room and returned with a pot of cold tea and poured me a cup. The cup was dirty and the tea sickeningly sweet, but I drank it down. The younger woman brought some pieces of bread and a bowl of raisins, and the old man broke the bread and held a piece toward me. Then he poured some tea for himself and his sons, and they passed the bowl of raisins around and sipped the tea.

"America!" muttered the older son. "It is said that every man there is wealthy—that all live in great houses like palaces and that each man has an automobile as large as a red-flag limousine."

"America is a rich place," I said.

"The brother of Mohammed Kharry once visited America," said the younger man. "He said that there women show their legs and paint their lips. He said that if a man wants a woman he does not need to marry."

I laughed. "Sometimes," I said. "Not always, but sometimes."

The younger woman blushed and the men laughed.

"Americans like hashish," said the older son with a sly smile. I had begun the game and had to play it through, so I nodded and smiled back at him. The two sons exchanged a glance; then the younger went to the other room. In a moment he returned with two pipes and a bag containing tobacco mixed with a chalky white substance. The pipes had long, curved stems and the bowls were made of clay. He packed them with the tobacco and lit one, drew on it until the bowl glowed, then passed it to me. I puffed. The tobacco was so strong that the taste of the hashish was barely noticeable. I let the smoke drift through my nostrils, trying to concentrate to keep the narcotic from confusing me.

The other pipe had been lit and the two younger men were passing it back and forth, each taking a big puff, then letting the smoke escape slowly through his nostrils.

After a half-dozen draws the room seemed very bright and the Uighurs strangely distinct. Their features were clear, yet they did not seem real. It was as if I could snap my fingers and they would vanish together with the room and the city, the police who wanted to arrest me and the security men who were following me, and the whole damned country with its eight hundred million people.

The old woman had gone to sleep, and the young boy lay beside his mother, curled up like a cat. The brothers sat cross-legged, lost in their reveries, and the old man was rocking slowly back and forth, chanting words I could not understand.

The young woman stared at me. Her eyes seemed enormous. Her brows were arched and in the half light of the room she looked like a goddess, proud and unafraid. An amused smile had turned up the corners of her mouth, and she took the pipe from me, knocked out the ashes, and refilled the bowl. By now the men had lain down and were sleeping the peaceful sleep that hashish gives. The woman took a stick, lit it in the oven, then handed it to me so I could light the pipe.

"You must go before the dawn comes," she said.

"Otherwise the neighbors will see. There are those who talk to the police."

I started to rise but she shook her head. "It is not time yet. Sleep, and I will wake you in the morning."

The child sleeping beside her stirred, and she stroked his head. I lay down and watched as she rose and walked to the switch that turned off the light. She was tall and slim and moved gracefully. Then the room was dark, and I heard her come back to the platform and lie down.

I closed my eyes and fell into a half sleep. Once I thought I heard the child whimper, then the voice of the woman soothing it. The next thing I knew, the woman was shaking my shoulder gently, and I rose and followed her to the gate and stepped out into the dark street. The gate closed behind me and I heard the bar drop into place; then I turned and walked quickly up the street toward the center of town, shivering as I went.

Chapter Seven

The first light of dawn was streaking the eastern sky with pink fire when I reached the hotel. I pushed aside the blanket that covered the doorway to the street and moved silently through the passageway to the courtyard and my room. My suitcase lay as I had left it, the blanket folded neatly at the bottom of the sleeping platform and a smouldering coal in the stove the only signs that someone had been in my room. The old man would have done this—it was his job. I inspected the lock on the suitcase. If it had been opened, whoever had done it had used a key. My clothes were folded as they had been when I closed the suitcase the night before. I hesitated for a moment, then quickly changed into western clothes. The icy water in the wash basin was like a tonic. I reached for the hotel towel to wipe the yellow paste off my face, then stopped and searched for my own. I wanted to leave no record of what I had done, no thread that could lead them back to me.

When I emerged from the passageway and headed toward where I thought the bus station lay, the main street was filled with early morning traffic. I walked briskly, feeling the stares of the people.

A sign outside the depot, chalked on an oily piece of

slate, said that the bus for the train station left at eight. I went inside to buy a ticket. When the people waiting saw a foreigner they moved back and cleared a space for me before the ticket window. The clerk made my change, then gestured that the bus lay outside and to the right. I thanked him and walked out into the dusty field.

People were spread about talking in groups. The air was cool, and the breath of the people rose like steam. Men were hoisting suitcases to the overhead racks of the buses. Children ran about laughing. I found the bus to the station, and a man carried my suitcase up the ladder to the roof of the bus, then offered me a piece of bread and a sip of the lukewarm tea he was drinking.

Soon a crowd had assembled, the door of the bus opened, and we climbed aboard. This time I had a seat between two old women. They stared at me, then cackled with laughter, showing their toothless gums. The driver climbed aboard and a moment later, with a lurch and rattle, the bus pulled out of the field and into the narrow twisting streets of the city. In a few minutes we had left the city behind and were bouncing over the pitted roadway that cut through the desert like a scarred black ribbon. In the distance I could see mountains. I felt the parcel the shopkeeper had given me beneath my shirt. Soon I would be on the train: two days and I would be in Beijing. Everything was on schedule.

At the train station I discovered that the express for Beijing was due at noon. I bought a ticket for a soft-berth compartment, and one of the female attendants led me to the special waiting room for foreigners.

There was no heat in the room, and I sat alone and sipped cups of hot water to keep warm. Through lace curtains—the only curtains I had seen so far in Xinjiang—I watched trains come and go. I wanted to go to sleep, but the cold and the worry that I might miss my train kept waking me.

A train rumbled into the station, and I watched as the Chinese tried to crowd onto the hard-seat carriages. Because no one would yield, a bottleneck was formed and the conductor had to hold the train.

The door of the waiting room opened again, and the station attendant came to me and asked to see my travel permit. I took out the yellow card and showed it to her. She looked at it for a moment, then left, taking it with her.

I looked at the clock: ten forty-five. It seemed as if time were crawling. Another train rolled into the station. I watched the conductors get off, followed by the passengers. Then the attendants began to clean the cars, splashing water on them and using great, long-handled brushes to scrub them clean. Two policemen appeared on the platform. They walked past the window of the waiting room and stopped about twenty feet away. I began to perspire. The parcel I had picked up in Turpan was pressed close to my chest by the sweater I was wearing. It felt like a time bomb, slowly ticking away toward the moment when it would blow me to smithereens.

A crowd of passengers rushed through the gate and made for the train. Now was the time. The policemen had turned their backs. If I was going to make a run for it I should do so in the crowd. I hoisted my suitcase and started for the doorway just as the attendant entered, followed by the two policemen. She showed them my travel permit and they studied it for a minute, then spoke with each other. They laughed, handed me back my permit, and left.

I sat down, my knees shaking. For another hour I stared out the window. When the Beijing train rolled in at noon I boarded it, ordered lunch, and then shut my eyes to see if I could catch up on my sleep.

Chapter Eight

I dozed through the afternoon, waking now and then to watch the desert roll past—hill after hill of gray-brown gravel peppered with lifeless shrubs. The sky was a cloudless blue, and sometimes in the distance I saw salt lakes shimmering. Once we passed a herd of camels, the herder with staff in hand standing like a sentinel atop a rise. In the evening the attendant took my order for dinner, and it came half an hour later. I was famished and ate two bowls of rice and a mountain of stir-fried celery and roast pork and curried beef. Then I ordered a bottle of beer and drank it slowly as twilight settled over the desert. Finally, with a last blaze of red, the sun sank and a million stars twinkled in a blue-black sky.

At nine thirty I left my compartment to stretch my legs. Behind my carriage were a dozen cars: first the hard-berth sleepers, then the carriages with only rows of hard wooden benches. These were jammed to overflowing. People sat on the floor and perched on small slats that folded down into the aisle. There was a constant hum: babies cried, men argued and played cards, old women played with their grandchildren and gossiped with their friends. When I passed, heads turned and children stared at me.

I walked to the end of the train where the sleeping car for the crew was, then started back toward my carriage. A conductor passed and nodded to me, then a young female attendant.

For a second we stared at each other. She was the same attendant who had brought me food on the train that had taken me into Turpan.

"The train stops at Hami at twelve," she said and I nodded, then went into my compartment, locked the door, unfolded a blanket, and crawled under it. Hami was near the eastern edge of Xinjiang; by morning we would be halfway through Gansu and well on our way to Beijing. The sound of the train clicking over the rails was soothing. I felt good. For a moment I thought of the attendant. She had to remember my mysterious exit from the earlier train. Perhaps she would alert the authorities. The thought should have frightened me but, oddly, it didn't. Instinct told me I was safe with her. Soon I fell into a deep sleep.

It must have been sometime soon after midnight when I was awakened by the sound of someone knocking on the door of my compartment. At first I thought I was dreaming, but the sound continued and I sat up, groggily reached for the light switch, then opened the door. The attendant was standing outside with a large Chinese man dressed in a heavy blue Mao coat and cap.

They came into the compartment, and the attendant took his ticket and handed him a plastic check from her roster of available seats and left. I lay back down and watched him stow his suitcase under the bottom berth and take off his shoes. Finally he switched off the light and crawled under the blanket.

I listened to try to tell if he was sleeping, but his

breathing did not change and I knew he was awake. He was probably only a passenger, and the attendant had probably put him in my compartment because the others were full, but it seemed to me that she had made an undue show of searching her clipboard for the plastic seat check—a show that had been intended for my benefit.

I must have drifted off because I was awakened out of a deep sleep by the reading light over the small table that sat under the window. The man was sitting at the table, reading a book and making notations in it. I looked at my watch: it was four A.M.

Sometime toward five I fell back into a half sleep that had almost become real when martial music from the speaker underneath the window woke me. A little later the attendant came to see if I wanted breakfast, and she and the large Chinese argued. Then she left. I took my shaving kit and went to find her, so that she could unlock the washroom for me. When I returned twenty minutes later, my breakfast was waiting on a tray, and the man and his suitcase were gone.

As I ate the toast and greasy fried eggs the attendant had brought me, I noticed that the sky had a peculiar cast to it—not the clear, pellucid blue that had persisted, day after day, in Turpan, but a milky, pearl color that darkened to gray far to the north.

I was finishing the glass of sweetened milk laced with thin, almost tasteless coffee, when the attendant reappeared to take the tray away. She waited patiently while I took a last swallow, then lifted the tray. As she did so, I noticed her eyes move to the window and the sky beyond. There was an anxious expression in those eyes.

I said the sky looked "dirty," which was the only word I could think of in Chinese to describe it.

She nodded and shook her head, her eyes remaining fixed on the horizon.

"Very bad," she said. "Rain comes here only a few times a year. The riverbeds are not deep. Sometimes when there is a storm there are great floods and many people die. It is very bad."

When she left she was still shaking her head. I leaned back and watched the desert pass. It was as rocky and barren as ever, though now I could see some mountains in the distance, like great sentinels beneath the lowering sky. The prospect of a flood seemed inconceivable to me. The land was a brittle crust of rock and sand, riddled with fissures where the crust had cracked in the sun's heat. It would soak up water like a blotter. I rummaged through my bag, looking for the novel I had bought just before I left Beijing. It was a detective story by an English writer I'd never heard of and wasn't very good, but it would help me pass the time. The parcel still lay under my shirt, where I could be sure of it. I patted it for reassurance, then started to read. I had completed five pages and was becoming faintly interested, when the first large rain drops splattered against the window.

Chapter Nine

The rain fell steadily, great pencil-shaped drops drumming against the roof and windows of the carriage. The sound was pleasant—it reminded me of home and summers I'd spent in a cottage on a lake in Connecticut, where it seemed to rain every afternoon at three. I watched as the sky grew darker and the rain increased, but still the attendant's worries seemed to me nonsense. There was not even the slightest sign of a puddle, let alone a swollen stream or river.

The train rolled on through the morning, and at noon the attendant reappeared, carrying a tray with my lunch on it. When she set it down I commented on the weather.

"It looks as if it will rain all day," I said.

She looked out the window, seeming to study the dark sky, and I noticed that her anxious expression had increased in intensity.

"Very bad," she said. "There are places ahead where the track crosses rivers, and the bridges are not strong—much water will wash them away."

I didn't think that I should disagree with her, so I nodded. She left and I continued to watch the rain fall. About three the sky began to brighten and the rain decreased. No flood, I thought, half in jest, and returned to the book I had started. By four the sky was almost blue and the rain had stopped. I rose and left my compartment and began to walk toward the rear of the train.

When I reached the final car—the one for the staff that was always kept locked—I stood in the vestibule between cars to feel the wind. There was no window here so I could not see the desert, but there was a space beside the walkway, and beneath it I could see the ties flashing backward in a blur. The click of the wheels was loud, but the cool air felt good, and my thoughts began to move forward toward Beijing. Even though the Chinese customs agents at the airport seldom did body searches, I would be a fool to try to take the parcel out myself. I would invoke that time-honored expedient, diplomatic immunity, and give the pick-up to the Canadian military attaché. He could put it in his country's diplomatic pouch.

The train seemed to be slowing, for the sound of the wheels clicking over the rails was softer, and I could see, vaguely, the outline of individual ties. I had turned and started for the doorway when, with a lurch, the train stopped, and I was thrown forward and slammed into the door. I heard shouts and then listened as the whistle was tooted four times; then the door of the staff car burst open and a dozen men rushed out, pulling their coats on as they did so. Three female attendants followed them. As they passed I asked the last one why we had stopped.

"The bridge!" she said. "It is gone!"

When I got back to my car the train was in chaos. The passengers were all pressed to the windows, and the attendants and conductors were guarding the doorways to make certain that no one got off. A group of men who looked like officials were huddled together in the dining car with a map spread on the table before them, and one man kept pointing to a certain place on it and saying something I couldn't make out. The others looked grave and kept shaking their heads. There was nothing else to do, so I went back to my compartment.

From the window the desert looked as it had before the storm—parched rock and gravel as far as the eye could see. If the rain had made the slightest difference I could not detect it. The mountains loomed in the distance, blue-gray walls of rock topped with snow. It could have been a scene from a western movie, and I almost expected Randolph Scott to ride into view, chased by a band of outlaws. Then I heard the clamor of voices growing louder. I opened the doors of my compartment and saw that the car was full of people from the hard-berth carriages. They were being held back by four of the conductors, but gradually they were pressing forward, moving toward the dining car and the officials. Their voices rose and fell in a constant din. One of the female attendants motioned that I should go back into my compartment, and I did so and locked the door. There was more noise and some shouts and then I heard the people push past, beating their fists on my door as they did so, and I knew that Randolph Scott had never ridden his horse into a world like the one I was in.

For an hour I stayed inside the locked compartment. The din outside quieted to a steady hum. In the background I could hear someone speaking to the crowd. It sounded as if people were asking him questions and he was responding. Then the crowd began to move again, past my compartment, back toward their berths and seats in the other carriages. After they had passed I waited a few minutes, then unlocked the door and stepped out. Three female attendants were standing beside the window, speaking to one another and looking disconsolately at the sky and desert beyond. When I approached, the attendant whom I knew turned and smiled shyly.

"When will we begin moving again?" I asked.

She listened intently to be certain that she understood, then said, with an expression of regret for something she could not help but somehow felt responsible for, "Not for a very long time. The bridge has been washed away."

"Perhaps they will send buses for us," I said.

"There is no road here," she replied. "Buses could not reach us."

"Perhaps then they will send army trucks," I added, wanting to cheer her up because she looked so distressed.

"Yes, maybe," she answered, but she did not look very certain.

"Well, at any rate we'll have a good rest," I said.

One of the attendants called, "Xiyou!" and she forced a smile and rejoined them.

When the sky turned crimson and orange in the west, I began to wonder vaguely when dinner would come. At six I expected a knock on my door, then at seven. Finally I went to look for Xiyou. A steady stream of people traipsed past the door of my compartment, heading for the dining car, and I joined them.

When I reached the car I found the people lined up, each carrying an aluminum tin. At the head of the line a cook in a greasy apron was ladling rice out of a giant pot, giving each person one ladleful. This filled their tins about one-third full.

Between my car and the hard sleeper I found Xiyou talking to two small children. She looked up—she was squatting to be on their level—and smiled at me.

"I have no tin for rice," I said. "Could you find me one?"

She led me back to my compartment, then told me to wait and she would return. In about fifteen minutes she was back, carrying a tray with a bowl of rice and some stir-fried pork and onions and a glass of tea.

"I am sorry, but this is all the cook has for today," she said. "He must save some food until we can continue on our journey."

She hesitated for a moment before leaving and stood at the doorway. There was something innocent in her expression that made me think of a nun who had taught me Catechism in the fifth grade. This girl had the same selfless grace about her.

"I am very worried," she said. "There are many people on the train and we are far from a town. There is only food and water enough for three days."

"I'm sure someone will come before that," I said. "The authorities cannot forget an entire train."

"There has been a great flood in Anxi," she said. "Many people have died, and there is no food or water in the town. It is over one hundred fifty kilometers to the next town, and there are no roads through the desert. We have no radio to tell the authorities where we have stopped."

"They can probably guess," I said. "After all, there can only be a few bridges."

"There are ten bridges," she replied. "And besides the bridges there are other places where a train might stop."

"Then we will just have to be patient," I said.

"Yes," she said, "that is what the leaders say."

When she had gone, I ate and then sat back to watch the last rays of the sun die out. The power had been shut off, so I could not read. Soon darkness would fall. Already it was cool in the compartment, and by midnight it would be freezing cold. I remembered my flight to Urumchi and the thread of track I had seen beneath us—one thin line in a vast brown carpet that seemed to stretch on to infinity. We were somewhere on that thread right now, but no one except the train's engineers knew exactly where. Then I scoffed at myself for worrying. They could always spot us from the air and fly food and water to us if need be. They could not just forget about an entire train. I shivered and took two blankets from the upper berth and crawled under them. It would be a long night, and I might as well get as comfortable as possible.

Chapter Ten

The sound of the wind, moaning softly as it drove the sand before it, woke me. I pushed back the curtain from the window. The night was pitch black—not even the moon was visible. I rose and unlocked the compartment door and went out. The aisle was deserted. At the far end there was a kerosene lantern that threw an eerie, flickering light about. The moan of the wind rose and fell, and somewhere another sound mixed with it.

When I opened the door to the next car I suddenly knew what the strange sound was. A whining din was emanating from the voices of the people who filled the car. They were spread about, some sleeping, others propped against the wall. A small crowd had gathered in a space before the tier of bunks near the center of the car. Several of them were bent over, looking at something that was happening on the bottom berth. I heard soft moans, the kind of sounds a person near death makes. In a minute the people separated and Xiyou emerged and walked past me.

I moved closer to see what the problem was. An old woman lay on the bed. Her face was drawn and her lips looked almost bloodless; she was blinking rapidly and kept opening and closing her hands. The people looked worried and one woman was crying. On the top berth opposite, three small children were staring down wide-eyed.

Xiyou came back carrying a small aluminum case with a red cross painted on it. She hunted through the case, then took out a bottle of pills and gave two to the old woman. Someone in the crowd lifted a cup of tea to the woman's lips. The woman coughed and the liquid trickled out of her mouth and ran down her chin.

Xiyou arranged some pillows under the woman's head, and someone covered her with a blanket. Then Xiyou rose, and, after saying a few words to the woman who was crying, she pushed through the people again and started back toward my car. I held the door open for her and she smiled tiredly and I followed her.

"The old woman is dying," she said, "and there is no one to nurse her. We have only very simple medicines and no one who understands how to use even them."

We had reached my compartment now and stopped. The flame in the lantern at the end of the car flickered wildly in the wind, making our shadows do a weird dance on the wall. She looked embarrassed, and I guessed she wanted to leave—probably go to bed—and that she did not know how to take leave of me.

"I shouldn't keep you from sleep," I said. "You look very tired."

"I don't want to sleep yet," she said. "I cannot because each time I close my eyes I begin to worry."

"That does no good," I said.

"I know," she said, and pushed down one of the small folding seats beneath the window in the aisle and sat. I did the same.

"It is worst at night," she said. "That is the time when I become the most worried."

I shivered and she looked at me with concern.

"You are cold. You should rest or you will become ill."

Coming from her the statement seemed incongruous, for she had spent the day working, while I had slept and stared out the window. But she forced herself to her feet and began to walk up the aisle toward the flickering lantern. Halfway there she suddenly crumpled and fell.

She said afterwards—after we had carried her to her bed and put her under some blankets—that she was merely tired, that was all. She was like that: she would work until she dropped unless someone stopped her. With other people she was a wonder—she knew just how much they could stand and never let them drive themselves over the limit—but with herself she was no judge.

By the next afternoon she was busy at work again. She looked pale, but when she passed me in the aisle she managed a smile. It was almost as though what happened the day before had embarrassed her—as if she would not allow herself to show the same weaknesses as those she ministered to.

Meals continued to come to my compartment. She did not bring breakfast and it came late, but lunch and dinner were on time and she brought them. The portions were small, but there was still meat with the rice. I asked her what the others were eating and how much rice was left.

"The cook is skillful," she said. "He can feed the people for two more days, perhaps three, but then there will be nothing."

I thought guiltily of the meat that I had just eaten and how hungry the children looked and how they cried.

"Couldn't men go on foot?" I asked eventually. "They could walk to the nearest town and summon help."

No, she said, that would be impossible. The distance was too far—no man could cross it without a camel, and even if he had a camel, a man who did not know the way would be more likely to perish than find the town.

"It is a small place, an oasis," she said. "Even those who have lived here all their lives are afraid to cross the desert. There is no road, no signs to mark the way. The wind blows the sand, and it is always shifting, so that the desert looks different each day."

"Surely they will send a plane to find us soon," I said. "Even now they are probably searching."

She nodded, but it was an act of politeness, not agreement. Another attendant passed and greeted her.

"Your foreign friend looks happy today, Xiyou," she said with a mischievous smile. "He was very sad when you were ill."

She was short and squat with a pretty face and a very direct, frank manner.

"Foreigners are always very tall," she said. "The last foreigner I met was over two meters. You are not so tall."

She continued to inspect me until Xiyou said, "The old woman was weak when I looked at her at eight. Someone should bring her some tea and gruel."

The girl nodded, giving me a smile that seemed part smirk, and walked off toward the dining car.

"Jen Ling is not polite," Xiyou said once her friend was out of earshot, "but she works hard."

I must have laughed because suddenly she smiled, and I felt myself begin to blush. For a second this disconcerted her, and she looked away to hide her confusion.

"I do not think we should worry so much," I said.

She gave me another of her forced smiles and said, "Once I was on a train in Mongolia. It was the middle of

February, and we stopped on the grasslands because the snow had blown over the tracks. The temperature was minus thirty. Many people were frightened, but luckily there were soldiers on the train and they kept order."

"And you survived," I added. "Surely that was a more dangerous place than here. It is not minus thirty here and there is no snow."

"That time the track remained under the snow," she said. "Once the wind had blown it away we continued on our journey. Mongolia is only a day's journey by rail from Beijing, four days by truck. Here we are in a desert that no trucks can cross, and we are a week's journey from the capital."

Now she looked worried again, and I began to wish I had not spoken, but suddenly her expression brightened, and she smiled and pointed out the window.

"There are people out there," she said excitedly. "I saw men on horseback in the distance."

I squinted in the direction in which she was pointing. A small row of dots had appeared on the far horizon.

"I must tell the others," she said, and rushed off.

I stood by the window and studied the dots. They moved steadily, weaving like a strange, beaded snake, up one hill, down, then up another. As they grew closer I could make out the faces of the men. They were Han dressed in the olive-colored uniforms of soldiers, with red tabs on their collars. When they reached the train they dismounted and walked in a group toward the cars. They looked tired and their clothes were covered with the thick yellow dust of the desert. Their horses were lathered and blown.

One man separated himself from the others, who squatted on the ground and waited while he boarded the train.

I was relieved to see the men, but at the same time had an uneasy feeling: none of the horses carried supplies. The man who had entered the train conferred with the conductor for a few moments, then was led to the dining car. I peered through the doorway and saw a dozen men gathered around him. They took out a map and studied it. Then someone summoned the soldiers from outside, and they entered the dining car and were given rice and tea. A little later Xiyou passed, and I stopped her and asked about the men.

"They came from Anxi," she said. She looked even more worried than before.

At noon Xiyou knocked on my door and entered, carrying a tray with my lunch. This time there was only a bowl of rice and some tea. She sat opposite me and watched as I ate.

"I am sorry," she said. "The meat that remains must be saved for the soldiers. They stay only for a few hours, then they must ride on to Yumenzhen. There is much need of them there."

"And us?" I wanted to say but did not.

She rose to go, and I noticed that she looked very pale and moved slower than she had before. Some people passed in the aisle outside, and someone called to her. She answered, then hovered at the doorway for a moment, as if she wanted to say something more.

"The situation is bad," she said. "The other passengers do not know this, and we do not want to tell them yet. But . . ." She looked out the window, toward the brown, trackless hills. "In Anxi the flood has driven the people from their homes. Liuyuan and Yumenzhen were also struck. There the damage is not so bad, but in Yumenzhen there is difficulty. There is no food and the people turn to old ways—looting and fighting. The soldiers go to stop those things. They cannot stay to help us."

There was more noise in the corridor, and again I heard her name called.

"I must go," she said, and left, sliding the door closed behind her.

The soldiers rode off in the afternoon, heading east. I sat at my window and watched them until they were out of sight. It took half an hour until the last dot had disappeared into the blur where the sky and the desert fused. Then I rose and went out into the aisle. Sitting had become irksome and I needed to walk.

When I reached the end of my car, I discovered that the door that led outside was open. Probably the soldiers had left by it. I went out.

The wind blew softly. It was a cold wind, but the sun was still high so it didn't chill me. All around, the sand seemed to be dancing, skimming inches above the ground in a fine spray. The paper-dry leaves of a few green-gray shrubs waved like streamers in the wind.

I shielded my eyes and stared off to the south. Very far away, the outline of mountains was vaguely visible, purple teeth against the blue sky. Anxi lay behind those mountains. It was over a hundred miles away, but it was the closest town, the one we would have to go to. I wondered how soon we would begin. It would be a hard journey but not impossible. The men and the strong women would survive, probably the strongest of the children too. But for the very old and the very young it would be impossible.

I looked down the length of the train. There were ten

cars, all except the dining car and my carriage filled to overflowing with people. I had no idea of the number—five hundred? a thousand? two thousand? It made no difference. We had to cross that desert.

I could see faces in the windows of the car closest to me. A little boy waved and I waved back. He looked very small in the window, and I wondered how old he was. Perhaps six or seven. He was probably one of those who would not survive the crossing.

Chapter Eleven

That night at eight while the sky was still bright in the west, there was a soft rap on the door of my compartment. I slid it open and Xiyou was there. I motioned that she should come in, and she did so, leaving the door open behind her.

She sat primly on the bottom berth opposite me, her hands clasped and held between her knees. She looked younger than before because her face was thinner. A few days had done that—worry and lack of food and sleep. I wondered how much she was eating; probably she was giving half her ration to others.

"It has been decided," she said. "Tonight the leaders speak to the people. At nine tomorrow we will begin the journey to Liuyuan."

"Anxi is closer," I said. "Why do we not go there?"

"There is nothing in Anxi," she said. "There the people beg for bread. They can feed no more mouths. Gansu is a poor province. Even in good years they do not have enough food."

I nodded, only half listening.

"It is not the fault of the leaders," she said. "Now things

are much better than they were before, but no one could have stopped the river from flooding."

"Perhaps one day they will build dams on the river," I said. "Then when the floods come they can be controlled. You have many people. With so many workers it would be easy to build a dam."

A look of anger that I had never seen before flashed across her face. It was as if I had touched a raw nerve. She rose and went to the doorway.

"Foreigners always think as you do," she said. "They believe that China's problems are simple—that all we need do is tell the people, 'Do this!' or 'Do that!' and it can be done. If it were that easy it would have been done before. Do you think our leaders are fools?"

I didn't respond, but this only angered her more.

"You come from a rich land, a land with many machines, with coal and iron and scientists and engineers. Only ten years ago China was a country filled with starving people."

There were tears in her eyes and her hands were shaking. She mumbled something I couldn't understand and left.

I tried to read but the evening light was too weak, so I gave up and looked out the window. The sky had darkened and a few stars were faintly visible. I shut my eyes but sleep would not come. I listened to the wind moaning across the desert. It rose and fell in a gentle, unending melody. In the car behind mine, children were sleeping, unaware of what lay before them. Let them sleep peacefully, I thought, for it will be a long time before they sleep so well again.

Chapter Twelve

Early in the morning we began our journey. Outside the cars people collected in a huge mass. I calculated that there were about two thousand. The leaders conferred for a few minutes, then walked off, leading the way. The people followed in a line, families walking together, wives and children and grandparents. There was a subdued joy in their faces—as if they were going on an outing. The children were happy to be out of the cars, the old people to be going to a place where they would have enough food. But on the faces of the men there was another expression: They were serious and walked with a steady, purposeful stride, their eyes fixed on the horizon.

We walked throughout the morning. The hills were steeper than they had appeared from the train. They were made of gravel and fragments of sharp, gray, slatelike stone that slid beneath our feet as we tried to climb. At first the people struggled up these hills in an upright posture, but soon they found this too difficult and climbed hunched over, using their hands like claws to gain purchase on the rocks. Sometimes small children fell, crying out as they slid or rolled down the hills. The old people had to be helped up the hills by the younger ones. Ropes were tied around their waists and they were pulled or pushed from behind.

By noon, when the sun was overhead and we stopped to rest, half the people looked too worn to go on. They squatted on the ground or stretched out, almost lifeless. Their clothes and faces were powdered with brown dust. Children cried and old people sat wheezing and coughing, their faces drawn and pale with the effort they had made. Each received some cold rice and a few swallows of tea, which the cooks dished out from a makeshift kitchen. They gobbled the rice greedily, but savored the tea, taking tiny sips to make it last.

Then everyone rested for half an hour before resuming the journey. I climbed to the top of a hill that seemed higher than the others and searched the horizon. The train lay behind us, perhaps ten miles back. It looked like a great, green snake stranded in a frozen ocean of brown waves. This ocean stretched all around, an endless grainy brown vista of hills with here and there a shrub or an outcropping of rock.

In the afternoon people began to slow down. The men, young women, and teenagers still walked steadily, but the children lagged behind and the old people were faltering. Finally several older women simply sat down. The leaders surrounded them, exhorting them to walk on but they refused, sitting mute and staring ahead into space as if the words being rained upon them were unheard.

The leaders held a meeting and decided to make camp for the day and build litters for the old people. A dozen men undertook this, stretching canvas between poles that had been used to carry sacks of rice and barrels of water. This meant that the remaining poles had to bear double the weight, and I wondered who would be given the impossible task of carrying them.

I stretched out and watched the sky. A few small clouds hung high up, almost in the stratosphere. The sky was pale and cold and the sun burned like a ball of white fire. While it shone, the air was warmed and the going comfortable. When darkness came it would be another matter. The desert was a cold place at night, especially when a man had no warm food in him.

As the sun sank slowly to the western horizon, the cooks prepared to dish out the rice and tea again. People crowded around their kettles and each received his portion. Still there was no panic or shoving, although the people's faces showed less confidence and more worry than before. Some of the children were crying but most seemed to have come through the day well enough.

I received my rice and tea and sat down to eat. Someone squatted beside me and did the same. I looked and saw Xiyou. She was eating in silence; she avoided my glance, finished her rice, and began to sip her tea. Then she spoke.

"I said words in anger last night. You must forgive me."

"There is nothing to forgive," I said. "You meant what you said and it was not wrong to say it."

"It is wrong to speak so to a guest," she replied.

She was struggling with her pride and her sense of etiquette. It was not easy for her.

"The desert is a hard place to walk in," I said, stretching my legs and rubbing my thighs.

"You are young and strong," she replied. "You should not complain. You must have led a soft life. Probably you worked in an office."

I decided that occupation was as good as any, so I nodded.

"If you were Chinese you would have been sent to the countryside to do physical labor. Then when you had proved you were a good worker you would be given a chance to return to the city and work in an office."

"I don't think I would have minded," I said. "My grandfather was a farmer. I like the countryside."

She gave me a look that showed she did not quite believe me.

"Some Westerners are farmers," I said. "We are not all rich bourgeoisie."

"You make fun of me," she answered.

"I'm sorry," I said. "You are a serious person and I am not so serious."

"For you life is easy," she answered, "and so you are cynical about China. You see the problems of my country, but you do not know how much good has been done in the last ten years or how much suffering lies in our past. My parents told me stories of the earlier times, of life under the warlords and the Kuomintang. You cannot understand what life was like then; no one who is not Chinese can understand. But it will do no good to speak to you of these things now." She sighed. "Perhaps later when you have learned more."

"Yes," I said, "perhaps later when we have reached Liuyuan and have rested and eaten a good meal."

She rose and walked off through the people. I watched her for a long while. Once she stopped to speak to some children, then to an old woman. Finally I lost sight of her in a crowd of officials all dressed in blue as she was.

▽

Chapter Thirteen

Night descended suddenly. First there was a golden glow in the west, the sky almost turquoise where the blue and yellow fused, then an orange glow, then pink, then, in a moment, total blackness punctuated with millions of twinkling stars. I had brought two blankets with me and wrapped myself in these. I was dead tired, and almost as soon as my eyes closed I was fast asleep.

It must have been shortly after midnight when I woke. The cold was piercing; it seemed to penetrate to the bone. I pulled the blankets more tightly around myself, trying futilely to manufacture some warmth, but it did not work.

Keeping my blankets wrapped around me, I rose and walked through the people until I came to the edge of the camp. From far off over the desert, somewhere to the north, there came a faint sound that puzzled me: it was like the roar of distant cannons.

I looked back toward camp. The ground was flooded in bright moonlight, and the people looked like a flock of sleeping sheep. Then the rumbling came from the north again, this time louder. The sky was still black but the air had come alive, as if filled with swirling smoke. The wind began to moan. At first it was a low hum, but in a few minutes it had increased to a loud, wailing shriek.

The sand whipped up by the wind cut into my face and I shielded my eyes. It bit into my skin, stinging like a thousand mosquitoes. I attempted to return to my place in the midst of the people, but when I tried to walk I was knocked down. Shrubs whipped past me, then small pieces of gravel. The moan grew louder. I curled into a ball and waited.

The roar increased. It sounded like a great jet revving its engines. The sand clogged my nostrils, my mouth. I gagged and gasped. The air seemed solid; it was impossible to tell where the ground ended and the air began, for the sand underneath me was moving too, sweeping away to the south in great sheets. I was torn loose, lifted, tossed like a rag. I thought I heard shouts and cries for help but could see nothing. I clawed at the shifting sand, trying vainly to find some way to secure myself. It did no good. I kept rolling and spinning about. Finally I realized that all I could do was protect my eyes and try to keep my nostrils and mouth unclogged.

The wind grew louder, beating against me until I ached. I felt the sand begin to cover me and I clawed it away from my face. Again it covered me, again I pushed it away. Even the air seemed to be screaming for mercy.

How long the worst of the storm lasted I don't know, perhaps half an hour, perhaps two hours. All sense of time vanished. I felt more dead than alive, and it seemed the wind would never stop, that it would grow louder and stronger until it destroyed the whole world.

When it died, it did so almost as suddenly as it arose. First the roar softened to a moan. The sand continued to blow, but the spray was finer and I did not have to struggle so to breathe. Then there was no sand, only the soft moan of the wind. Then silence.

I stood. The sky was as clear as before. The stars twinkled. The desert looked the same. I felt under my shirt. The papers I had picked up in Turpan were still there, but the breast pocket of my shirt where I kept my passport was empty. All around me I could see the shapes of other people doing as I was, struggling to their feet and rubbing their eyes to clear them of sand. Some brushed their clothes off. Then came the first cry of a mother calling for her child; then another cry and another. Soon the air was filled with shrieks and screams.

People rushed about, crying out the names of their children. The moon was bright and for perhaps a hundred yards around I could see almost as clearly as in daylight. There were no children in sight. An old couple lay about ten feet from me, the woman on her side; she did not appear to be breathing. The man struggled into a sitting position and then rocked back and forth, moaning softly. Otherwise all I saw were younger men and women and a few teenagers.

Soon the cry reached a fever pitch, and the leaders appeared and called the people together. They formed a mob around four men, who spoke to them for several minutes; then the people fanned out and began searching for the children to the south of the encampment. After fifteen minutes the first body was discovered. This was a small girl, lying on her side as if asleep. A woman rushed out of the crowd and clutched her to her breast, then began to weep. The child looked peaceful. If you did not look closely you could not tell she had stopped breathing.

Now bodies were discovered in rapid succession—an infant, two girls of about seven or eight, a boy of ten. The infant was dead; one of the girls was still breathing. The boy appeared to be all right.

The hunt went on throughout the night. When the first light of dawn broke, almost all the children had been accounted for. Over fifty had perished. Others coughed convulsively, gasping for breath through sand-clogged nostrils.

The cooks made tea and the people drank this and ate their cold rice; then they resumed their hunt. By noon the bodies of only two children remained missing. Both were from the same family. The leaders called another meeting, and the people were told to rest for an hour before resuming their journey.

When the sun was almost straight overhead they started toward the northwest again, moving slowly, like worn pack animals. At the very end of the column came the parents of the children who had not been found. The woman kept stopping and turning back. Each time her husband would pull her back into the column. After a mile had been traversed, I climbed to the top of a hillock and looked back. The hills of sand and gravel and rock stretched behind us, seemingly into infinity. Now even if we had wanted to, we could never have found the place where we had camped in the night. The landscape was all one great amorphous sea of shifting sand and gravel, caressed by the pitiless wind.

Chapter Fourteen

We walked until night fell. The going seemed easier now. We no longer had the weakest children to slow us, and the hills seemed less steep, the sand less shifting and treacherous. The great wind had blown the loosest sand away, leaving the ground rocky and almost bare in places. The sky was clear, and when night came the stars glittered like diamonds.

I savored each grain of the rice I was given, then sipped my tea. No one spoke. All seemed numbed by the tragedy of the night and the hard journey. When I had finished I lay on my back.

"You are studying the heavens," said a voice nearby. "Do you think you can read your fate in the stars?"

"No, Xiyou," I said. "I was just remembering other skies I had seen and other times when I slept without a roof above me."

"I have often slept like this," she said. "When I was young I went with my parents to Yunnan Province. In the summers it was hot and we slept in buildings with no walls, only screens. At night I would study the stars."

We said nothing more for several minutes.

"Are your parents still in Yunnan?" I asked at last.

"No," she answered. "They live in Beijing. My father is a cadre, my mother works in the Ministry of Hydro-electric Power."

It seemed strange to me that she was a conductor on a train. She should have had a more important job.

"I was a very poor student," she said, as if intuiting my unasked question. "All students who want to attend the university must take an exam. I have never done well on exams."

"Some would have used the back door," I said.

"There is no back door to the university," she replied. I chuckled and she snapped out, "For some things we have a back door—no one denies that—but to enter the university one must do well on the entrance examination. If not, he must go to the countryside or the factory and work for a period. Then he may try again."

"Will you try again?" I asked.

"I don't know," she said. "My job is a pleasant one. I have no wish to study now."

A baby began to cry nearby, and I rose on one elbow to see where the sound was coming from. About twenty feet to my right a woman had lifted a child to her breast and was nursing it.

"You ask many questions about me," said Xiyou, "but say nothing for yourself. Why have you come to our country?"

"I came as a tourist," I said, knowing that was the best answer because it opened me to the fewest troublesome questions.

"You must be a wealthy man," she said, "for it costs much for a foreigner to travel in China."

"I am not wealthy," I said.

The woman removed her breast from the baby's mouth and immediately it began to cry again.

"The child is hungry," Xiyou said. "His mother has no milk to give him."

"Liuyuan is still far," I said. "More will become hungry."

"The leaders say we can reach it in three more days," she replied.

I shook my head.

"Will many die?" she asked suddenly, surprising me with the directness of her question.

"If we reach Liuyuan in three days, most will live," I answered. "But we will not do that."

"But the leaders say we will," she replied.

"I think the leaders are wrong," I answered.

I slept poorly that night, for the cold kept me awake. Each time I began to fall asleep I would shiver back to consciousness. I thought of what I would have been doing if I had been back in the States. Probably lying in a soft bed. The air would have been comfortably warm and I would have been sleeping deeply, dreaming of the next day and what assignment I would receive. Or perhaps of the night before, my last adventure—a thigh or a breast, the smell of perfume, a mouth twisted in a half smile. That was what my life consisted of. It was pleasant enough, I guessed. I made a comfortable salary, had a nice car, saw attractive women, slept with some of them. Each year I paid my income tax and bought a few suits, took a vacation in the Caribbean, read a few books. Time was passing and I was moving slowly toward that magic number of twenty, which would mean I had accumulated enough years of service to retire. Then I would go south, perhaps the islands, maybe Mexico. Former agents lost themselves there, in towns with names like Los dos Amigos and Ciudad del Carmen. The locals thought they were retired businessmen; the resident Americans invited them to join their bridge clubs, to go golfing, to sail on their yachts. Everyone had a past there, but no one spoke of it. I would hire a pretty maid. I would build a swimming pool. Already I could imagine the feel of the sun, the taste of the drink the maid—she would be slim and shy and beautiful—would bring me.

Dawn came and I finally dozed off, numb with cold but too tired to resist sleep. It seemed that my eyes closed and a minute later I heard voices and the sound of people collecting their gear and the crying of hungry children. I rose and brushed the sand from my clothes. Already the sun was at an angle of fifteen degrees. It was past eight. I could see the cooks attaching the pot they boiled the rice in to the pole that enabled it to be transported. That meant I had missed breakfast and would have to wait for lunch for a drink and some nourishment.

When I stood, my weakness surprised me. My knees seemed made of rubber and I felt light-headed. I pulled myself together and began to walk. This will pass, I thought, but it didn't, so I sat down again.

The column had begun to form and from my cross-legged position I watched the adults collect their children, then their grandparents. One of the leaders gave a signal and they began to walk. I lurched to my feet and followed, moving unsteadily but keeping pace. Lights danced in front of my eyes and there was a strange buzzing in my head. My arms and legs felt detached. They had a will of their own and moved slowly. After a quarter of a mile I put my hand to my forehead. I was dripping with sweat.

The morning dragged on. People passed, staring at me as they did so. My steps grew slower. Finally I stopped and sat.

Something I could not understand was happening. Missing one meal could not account for the way I felt. I tried to struggle to my feet again, then gave up. The column was drawing away—already the last person was almost fifty yards ahead of me. I gave a feeble cry but no one heard; then, in a blur, I saw a figure separate from the column and move back toward me. I waved, trying to signal, to beckon. Lights flashed in front of my eyes, then everything went dark.

When I woke, Xiyou was holding a cup of cold tea to my lips. I swallowed greedily, and she pulled it away.

"Slowly," she said. "You do not need to drink it all at once. There is more if you need it."

I reached for the cup again, and she held it to my lips. The tea seemed to damp down the fire that was burning in my stomach, but it did nothing for the fire that was consuming my entire body. I tried to struggle to my feet, but she shook her head and held me down. It took hardly any effort for her to accomplish this.

"You have a fever," she said. "You must wait until it passes. Then you can walk again."

"But the column!" I exclaimed.

"The column has gone ahead. We will rejoin them when you are stronger. They move slowly. We can rest now."

"How long have I been here?" I asked.

"Four hours," she said.

The sun was still far above the horizon. If we hurried we could rejoin them by nightfall. Again I tried to rise.

"You are foolish," she said, frowning. "You cannot walk more than a few hundred yards without collapsing. Save your strength so that you can walk tomorrow. Otherwise we will never be able to rejoin the column."

I gave up and relaxed. She went away for a minute, then returned with a tin of rice and fed me some. As I ate I could feel my strength return.

"Now you will sleep," she said when I had finished, and she covered me with a blanket. I did as I was told.

When I woke, the sun had set. Xiyou was sitting about twenty yards from me, on the highest point of the hillock we were resting on, staring toward the west. She had curled into a ball and was resting her chin on her knees. She turned and looked toward me and smiled.

"You have slept soundly," she said. "That is a good sign. The fever has broken. Tomorrow we will continue the journey."

I wondered what had been said when I fell—who decided that someone should stay behind with me and how it was decided that she should be the one.

Two clouds drifted across the western sky, forming a crown above the moon. The desert was absolutely still, bathed in a silver light. The scene was indescribably beautiful—that we were alone and over a hundred miles from the nearest town hardly seemed to matter.

"I have never seen the desert like this before," she said, still staring off toward the horizon.

She rose and came toward me, walking slowly, sat close to me, and studied my face, as if it were a map of a new country that she was visiting for the first time.

"You are not as hard as you think," she said at last. "You still believe the lies you have been taught, but you have some generous impulses."

"In the West we would say 'his heart is in the right place,'" I said.

She smiled a very tired smile and lay down. In a minute

her eyes were closed and she was sleeping deeply, a look of peace on her face. In the stillness I could hear her breathing. The sound filled me with calm. Soon I slept too.

Chapter Fifteen

I was awakened by a gentle nudge. Xiyou was kneeling beside me, holding a cup of tea in one hand. She looked rested and had pulled her hair back and wiped the dust from her face.

"Drink this and eat some rice. Then we will see if you can walk," she said.

When I had finished I felt stronger.

"Come!" she said. "You must try to walk."

"I am waiting for you to eat your breakfast," I said. "Then we can begin."

"I have already eaten," she replied, and lifted a pack containing what remained of our rice and tea over her shoulder.

She was lying, but I knew it would do no good to argue. I resolved that she would eat lunch or I would not.

We moved slowly at first, for my legs were still weak, and several times I lost my balance; then, after an hour or so had passed and the sun warmed me, I began to feel my strength returning. Up one hill, down, then up again. We moved at a steady, even pace, walking side by side.

Her resilience amazed me. I had been ill but, still, I was in good condition; yet she kept pace with me easily. When we stopped it was I, not she, who did so. Then she would sit calmly while I caught my breath. She always kept her eyes on the horizon, as if searching for something there.

"How far ahead do you think the column is?" I asked.

"They have a day's lead on us," she said, "but in one day they cannot cover more than twenty kilometers. We should sight them by late tomorrow or early the day after."

"By that time they will be near Liuyuan," I said, as if it were a fact to be accepted.

"Yes," she said, and stood. I scrambled to my feet and we walked on.

That night we continued walking even after the sun had set. The moon was bright and the way clear. We rested once, at sunset, ate a handful of rice each and drank a few sips of water; then she stood up and beckoned me to continue.

"We have much ground to cover," she said as I lurched to my feet, groaning as I did so. "We can walk for three more hours."

My legs ached but I did as she wanted. When we finally stopped I collapsed and lay as if dead. She stood over me and laughed.

"Your life of automobiles and soft beds has corrupted your body," she said. "You should have been sent to the countryside for a month each year. Then you would not be so tired."

"We have no need for people in the countryside," I answered. "Our farms are cultivated by machines. In my country men leave the countryside to come to the city where there is work."

"And so you are corrupted," she said with a malicious

smile. "You sit behind a desk and order the workers to sweat so that you may eat your bread."

I gave her a sour look, and she shrugged, and I could see her lips begin to form the word 'bourgeois.' But then she stopped and looked away. We were both too tired to argue.

I rose and walked to the top of the hillock, while she sat in her usual pose, curled into a ball with her chin resting on her knees. When I reached the top of the hill I stared off across the desert to the northwest, hoping futilely that I would see a brightening of the sky—a sign that we were approaching Liuyuan. But there was nothing. The stars twinkled as before, like jewels against a cloth of the blackest velvet.

I wondered how the column was faring. It was now four days since they had begun their trek. Their rice and water would be nearly gone. They had begun at a good clip, averaging about fifteen miles a day, but they could not have maintained that pace—not unless they left the old people and the children behind. We had encountered no stragglers so far, so this possibility seemed unlikely. It was more probable that they had slowed but remained together. In that instance they could not be far ahead.

I shivered in the cold. I had not fully recovered, and the few handfuls of rice I had eaten in the past few days were hardly enough to keep up my strength. It did no good to think of the situation as it was, because then panic would set in, and panic incapacitates a man.

I was worried about Xiyou. She had been going too strong. Her political speeches were becoming more strident: that was to cover the fear she felt. She had not drunk half the water I had, and I did not know if she was eating any rice or not. The leaders would have given her no more than the usual ration for two people: they would be scrupulous in the matter. What she had been giving me was not adequate, but she was still probably skimping on what she was saving for herself.

I sat down beside her and we watched the stars together. Her eyes looked tired and the skin on her face was dry and creased with lines.

"We still have many kilometers to walk," she said. "Perhaps tomorrow or maybe early the next day we will sight Liuyuan. The column must have arrived already."

I looked at her incredulously.

"There are not many lights in the town," she said. "That is why we see no glow on the horizon. If it were a large town like Urumchi or even Hami we would see lights."

"Yes," I said, nodding mechanically. If she needed the illusion I did not want to destroy it.

Suddenly I heard a muffled sob and saw that she was pressing her forehead against her knees, trying to stem the sobs that were growing in her throat.

"It is bad," I said after a few minutes, "but we will be able to make the crossing. Already we are halfway and we are both still strong. Tomorrow after we have eaten you will feel differently. The hunger and thirst weaken one's courage—that is worse than the physical danger."

She raised her head and looked at me. There were two lines on her cheeks where tears had run over the thick layer of dust, leaving tracks behind.

"There is no more rice and water," she said. "We had the last of both at midday."

She pressed her head to her knees again and continued sobbing. I reached over and put my arm over her shoulder, and she rested against me. She felt light, almost like a child, and each sob seemed to shake her entire frame. We stayed like that for a long time. Finally she fell asleep and I covered her with the blanket and lay down beside her. Just before I fell asleep I felt under my shirt for the parcel that had brought me to this place. It was still there, like the albatross that had haunted the ancient mariner.

Chapter Sixteen

We began the next morning, walking steadily. Our pace was the same as it had been for the past three days, but I knew it would not last. At noon we stopped to rest for only half an hour, but when we started our trek again the difference was immediately noticeable. Xiyou struggled gamely, but she was faltering and she knew it. I could feel the strain in my legs, the slow drain of energy that would not be replenished. For a while I could continue, but not for long.

When the sun set we stopped. We had covered a few miles, not more. We sat, listless, and looked at the sky. We were both too weak to go on and too filled with fatigue to sleep.

"Tomorrow we will do better," she said. "We will feel better after resting."

I did not want to answer. Even the pretense seemed a farce to me. Better to accept the situation. If I was going to die I wanted to do it honestly, without any illusions.

Xiyou's eyes were fixed on the horizon. For an hour we sat, like two Buddhas, staring into space.

"I feel sorrow only because of my parents," she said at

last. "They will be saddened when I die. They will endure but they will not be the same."

"They will consider you a hero," I said. "They will be proud."

"My parents do not believe in heroes," she replied. "They have seen too much to believe that a man can be more than human. Before Liberation they lived in Nanking. Have you heard of Nanking?"

I remembered what I had read of the Japanese invasion and the accounts of the slaughter and rape of the Chinese populace.

"My mother saw her own mother and sisters raped, then killed by the rapists. My father was luckier. A bomb destroyed his home—he was the only survivor. In those days there was no party structure and the government did not provide for refugees. Both my parents had to find food and shelter without help. They lived through an entire year like hunted animals, fleeing from place to place, shivering in the cold, nearly starving. China was in disorder. They could turn to no one.

"My father joined the Communists. Twice he was nearly captured. All of his friends were killed. Those of his family who had not been killed by the Japanese were killed by the Kuomintang. Even today he rarely speaks of those times. For years he was unable to sleep at night, for each time he closed his eyes the painful memories would return."

I was becoming drowsy, and I felt my eyelids droop. Xiyou looked over at me and smiled; her teeth glittered in the moonlight.

"When you are tired you look like a very small boy. Did you know that?"

I said that I didn't.

"It is then that I can see that even if you have been corrupted you are not wholly corrupt."

"There is still hope for me, then," I said with a yawn.

"Yes," she said. "There is still hope."

The moon was high overhead. It shone down on us like a weak, silver sister of the sun. The stars formed a great net of sparkles, a vast world that glimmered and glowed. And beneath stretched the desert, dark and silent and endless. Xiyou finished speaking but remained as before, her chin resting on her knees. She was still in that position when I fell into a deep, dreamless sleep.

In the morning I woke first. The sky was tinted with crimson in the east, the air absolutely still. Overhead the North Star was still visible. I stretched and stood, looking toward the northwest. The sky was still dark in that direction. I strained my eyes, hoping against hope that I would see some sign of the column or the city we sought. But there was nothing. Only the hillocks of brown gravel and rock stretching on to the horizon.

My throat was dry and the skin at the corners of my mouth had split. But I could still stand and my legs felt strong enough for me to walk. That was a good sign.

Xiyou looked very weak but managed to struggle to her feet. Then we moved off, walking slowly, our heads bent, shuffling our feet in short, mechanical strides. We will do it! I kept thinking. If only we can keep moving we will do it!

But we could not. After an hour Xiyou had to stop. She did not ask for a rest or signal that she needed one—her legs simply stopped moving. Still she made the movements with her arms and tried vainly to push one foot ahead and pull the other after, but she moved slower and slower until she was almost standing still.

"We should rest," I said. I did not want her to know the truth—that she was holding us back.

We sat side by side. She was breathing hard, as if she had been running a race, but there was no sweat on her face because she had almost no moisture left in her body. Her eyes were bloodshot and a trickle of blood came from a place where her lip had split. I wiped it away and she made a feeble attempt to smile.

"We should start again soon," she said. "If we sit we will grow stiff. You will have to forgo your corrupt bourgeois ways and force your tired body to move."

"We can afford to rest for a short while," I said. "Then we can walk until dark."

She frowned but continued sitting. I rested and stared at the horizon, where the pale blue midwinter sky met the desert. When I looked at Xiyou again her eyes were closed and she was sleeping, breathing with the short, almost painful gasps of someone tired beyond her strength. There was no point in waking her. I shut my eyes and tried to sleep too.

I was awakened by a soft nudge in the ribs.

"We have been sleeping too long," she said. "The sun is almost at the horizon. We must walk."

I pushed myself to my feet and watched as she struggled futilely to do the same. The scene would have been comic if the circumstances had been different. She struggled, then fell back, then struggled again, but she simply could not rise. Finally I reached down and pulled her to her feet.

"My muscles are stiff from resting so long," she said, almost as if she were reproaching me for having allowed her to sleep.

We set off again. First the way led downhill for a distance of about forty yards. She managed this well enough, half sliding, half walking. Immediately we had to climb again. I knew she would have difficulty, so I followed her, and when she slowed I pushed her as I had seen the men do their grandparents while we were still with the column. Finally we reached the top of the hill and paused. We were both breathing heavily.

"You should go on," she said. "I am holding you back. Alone you have a chance."

I shook my head.

"I can go no farther," she said again. "You must go on alone."

I took her arm and we began to descend the hill. Twice she stumbled and almost fell. At the bottom we paused, then started up another hill. Her legs gave out and she fell, and I tried to lift her but she shook her head. "I cannot!" she said.

"Crawl!" I commanded, and she began to do this, me beside her. When we reached the top we collapsed and lay like two exhausted animals.

"It is no use," she said, her voice a hoarse whisper.

"We will rest and then we will start again," I said. "You will get some of your strength back."

She tried to laugh but only a grotesque gurgle came out, abbreviated by a spell of coughing. I raised my head and looked at her. Her eyes were half shut and her mouth open as she struggled for air. I reached over and brushed the sand from her face, and she smiled.

"Your bourgeois life has not weakened you as much as I had thought," she whispered.

"It is the rice you gave me and did not eat yourself," I answered. "Even a Communist needs rice."

She managed a chuckle, then shut her eyes. At least her breathing had slowed. She will sleep, I thought, and wondered if she would waken. It would be best that way—just to drift off painlessly.

I rolled over and stared at the sky. Night had almost fallen. The sky was still blue to the west, but overhead it was already turning purple. A few stars were visible. Once I had heard that if you wished on the first star of evening your wish would come true. Right then it seemed like our only hope.

The icy wind cut into me, peppering my face with sand. I rose on an elbow and, shielding my eyes, peered off across the desert. There was no way of telling what time it was, for the sun was completely hidden in a yellow-brown haze that covered the sky like a thick blanket. I reached out and felt Xiyou beside me. She was still breathing, but her breathing sounded shallow and irregular. I wrapped the blanket around both of us, trying to use our bodies to generate some warmth. She moaned softly but did not waken.

The wind howled louder, rising to a wail. Time passed, perhaps half an hour, possibly longer. The air became a swirling mass of sand; then, gradually, the wail softened. It was still freezing cold but the air was no longer filled with flying sand. I brushed the sand away from my eyes and looked across the desert.

The wind had come from the northwest, the direction in which they were headed. Now in place of the thick yellow haze the air was as clear as glass. I blinked. It seemed impossible and I rubbed my eyes. But my ears told the same tale. From out of the horizon came several large trucks, heading directly toward us. I scrambled to my feet and began to leap up and down and shout.

The trucks were still a quarter of a mile away, but they had sighted me, for the first truck turned slightly and climbed up a hillock, down, then up again until it stopped twenty feet from us. Two men climbed out and walked toward us. They were dressed in the tan uniforms of the People's Liberation Army.

They carried Xiyou to the truck and I followed them; we were placed in the back, under a canvas roof, and the truck started again, turned, and headed back toward the northwest. A man sat with us. He offered me some water, then gave some to Xiyou. She swallowed spasmodically, choked, then swallowed again.

I wrapped a blanket around her, then sat back against the side of the truck. It lurched as it climbed up and down the hills, and I was tossed back and forth roughly, but it made no difference. In fifteen minutes I was sleeping soundly and did not waken until we stopped in the center of Liuyuan.

Chapter Seventeen

I slept the sleep of the dead that night, woke early, rolled over, and slept again. Finally, toward noon, hunger drove me from my bed. I had been placed in a room of what looked to be a hotel. The walls were of mud brick, the floor flagstone. In the corner was a small stove with a flue that exited through a hole in the window.

I pushed back the blanket that covered the doorway and blinked as I emerged into the bright sunlight of midday. The town was small—the edge of it perhaps a mile and a half from the hotel, which appeared to be centrally located. About half a mile to the west the buildings ended and a series of hills covered with green shrubs began. Here I could also see a switching yard and a number of railroad sidings. The buildings in the town were a sorry lot—low, built of mud brick, separated by alleyways. They looked much poorer than those I had seen in Turpan.

After a few minutes I went inside and lay down again. There was nothing to tell me where I was or what I should do. I wondered where Xiyou was, but there was no one to ask.

Toward the end of the afternoon a tired-looking doctor arrived to examine me. He was chubby with gray hair and the wry, cynical expression often worn by Han Chinese who find themselves placed by their government somewhere they would rather not be.

After he took my pulse and listened to my lungs and asked about my stool, he pronounced me fit and started to leave. I asked him about Xiyou, but he shrugged. He had not seen her but guessed that she would be in the hospital that was located on the north side of the town. We went outside and he pointed off toward a large gray building with a roof of rusted tin. Then he remounted his bicycle and peddled off slowly down the street, moving as if he did not really want to arrive at the next place on his rounds.

I started off toward the hospital. There was no one in sight who could give me directions, so I had to depend on luck and intuition. Each street looked the same—filled with row after row of one-story houses built of mud bricks. Open sewers ran down the sides of most of the streets. Here and there were piles of garbage.

Finally I turned a corner, and there lay the hospital. From a distance it had appeared to be a low building like the rest, but now, up close, I saw that it was three stories in height. Its walls were of gray concrete, and the windows that had once been filled with glass were now mostly covered over with cardboard or cloth. A great central door opened into a vaulted hallway that led to the interior of the building. People filled the hallway, some standing, others squatting or sitting with their backs pressed to the wall.

I found a nurse and asked about Xiyou. She knew nothing and recommended that I ask someone else. I did this and the result was the same. Then I began wandering up and down the hallways, peering in through each doorway as I went. At the very end of the hall, near a doorway that led into the refuse-filled courtyard that lay behind the building, I found her.

She was sleeping when I entered. I sat on a chair, the only piece of furniture in the room except the bed. The walls were bare, the floor concrete. A lone window with three panes of glass and three pieces of wax paper opened to the courtyard.

Her face was pale. There were purplish circles under her eyes, and her lips were still cracked at the corners. She looked terribly ill, and suddenly I became very afraid for her.

I sat beside the bed and watched her sleep. Sometimes I dozed. Time passed and the shadows crept across the courtyard behind the building. Toward four she stirred and opened her eyes. When she saw me she did not look surprised, but smiled and then shut her eyes again. At six when they brought her evening meal, she finally woke. I wanted to stay, but she insisted that I leave so that I could find something to eat in one of the nearby restaurants. Afterward, she said, I could return and we could talk.

The sun had not yet sunk when I left the hotel and started up the street. A nurse had told me that a restaurant lay at the end of it; this was the only restaurant in the town, she said. There was something strange in her expression when she spoke that unsettled me.

It took me a while to locate the restaurant because all the buildings looked the same and there was no sign, not even the usual slate with items and prices chalked on it. Finally I saw a window with a light in it and peered in. There were a half-dozen tables spread around and people sitting at them. I went in and sat and a man came over. He was short and had a round yellow face. I asked what food there was and he said, "myfan"—rice. I said I wanted a bowl and a glass of tea. Five minutes later he returned with the rice and the tea. The rice was old and the tea weak, but I ate like a famished rat and asked for more rice. The man shook his head. I started to argue, then looked at the others in the restaurant. Their eyes were fixed on me with strange, unsettling stares. I paid and left quickly.

When I reached the hospital again, most of the lights had been switched off. The passageway to the inner courtyard was lit with a single bulb that glowed weakly. Inside the building, in the hallways, it was completely dark. I found the door of Xiyou's room by feel—I had remembered that it was the last in the hallway—and knocked. A soft voice answered from within, and I entered.

There was a candle flickering in a dish that had been set on the floor beside the bed. I sat and she smiled up at me and asked if I had eaten.

"Rice and tea," I said. "There is little food in the town."

She nodded. "The people are starving. They make do on a handful of rice every few days. It has been so since the flood, and day by day it becomes worse. But the government will send food soon."

She sighed, and I watched her face in the flickering light. Her eyes were closed with fatigue and her cheeks sunken. Her lips were still cracked at the corners of her mouth. A few oranges or an onion would have changed this—even the wretched vitamin C pills that the doctors prescribed.

From the hallway came the sound of footsteps and voices; then the door opened and three doctors entered. They looked surprised to see me but said nothing. One went to the bed and felt Xiyou's pulse. Another studied her chart. A third merely stood, staring vacantly ahead. They looked very tired. The man taking the pulse said something that I couldn't understand and the others nodded; then he listened to her lungs with a stethoscope and pushed down her lower eyelids and examined her eyes. Then the men nodded to me and left. I waited for a moment, then followed them.

They had gone into the room next to Xiyou's—I could see the light flickering through the open door. After a few minutes they emerged, and I approached them and asked about Xiyou. They looked confused for a moment. Then the doctor who had examined her motioned to me and we walked off together up the hallway so that we were forty feet or so from her room.

"She is very ill," he said when we had stopped. "She has no strength and there is congestion in her lungs. Her heart is very tired: it beats irregularly."

"Is there nothing that can be done?" I asked, already knowing the answer.

"If we had medicine . . . and if there was food," he said, "but—" He shrugged and shook his head.

"Can I do anything?" I asked.

"Watch over her," he said. "We have few nurses. Most have gone to the countryside to help in the villages. There is starvation everywhere. Typhoid, cholera . . ." His voice trailed off and he shook his head again. He was a small man with thick spectacles. His eyes were kind but they were very tired.

"Why doesn't the government send help?" I asked. "Why don't they send medicine and food and more doctors?"

"The government!" he said. Then he looked me directly in the eye and frowned. "To send supplies, trucks are needed and soldiers to drive them. We are not in Beijing, where there are many soldiers and trucks. Here the soldiers are all to the north and to the west. They guard the borders so that the Russians will not overrun us." He gave a bitter laugh. "Few men can be spared for something as unimportant as a flood."

We walked together back toward Xiyou's room.

"If she becomes faint, find us quickly," he said. "We still have some medicine to regulate the heartbeat, but it can be used only for emergencies."

"Is there nothing else I can do?" I asked.

"Find some food for her," he replied, and motioned to his colleagues, and they entered the next room.

Chapter Eighteen

I stayed with her most of the night. It became cold toward midnight, but I merely pulled my coat around myself more tightly. I dozed, woke, then dozed again. When my back became too sore I left the chair and lay on the floor. Every hour or so I rose and checked to make certain that she was all right. Her breathing continued to be regular, so I assumed she was okay. There were no other signs I could go on.

Morning finally came. She had weathered the night and looked no worse than she had the day before, and I began to feel optimistic. About eight the orderlies came with a cup of tea and half a bowl of rice. I watched her eat. She seemed to be reading my thoughts, for she said, "I know it is little, but it is more than most have. If there were more rice I would be given more."

I rose.

"You are going for breakfast?" she asked. There was something plaintive in her voice that I had never heard before, and suddenly I realized how afraid she must be.

"I will return soon," I said. "I must eat and see some men in the town. Perhaps"—I hesitated, afraid to speak of what I could not be certain of—"I will return with some food."

She looked at me and smiled the smile of the true believer.

"There is no food in Liuyuan—if there were, it would be used to feed the sick."

I nodded and left.

The streets were crowded with thin, hungry-looking people. They moved slowly, almost in a trance. Here and there someone was carrying a bucket of water, but otherwise everyone was empty-handed.

I walked toward the restaurant I had entered the night before. The door was open and one man was sitting at a table. I went in, and again the waiter came to me. This time when I asked what there was, he said only, "Cha"—tea. I asked for a glass, and when he brought it I took out the roll of bills from my pocket and peeled one off, making certain that he could see the pink flash of the fifty-yuan bills. His eyes met mine, and he took the money, then returned with the change. When he handed it to me, there was a note with it.

I drank the tea slowly, watching people pass on the street. Then, nonchalantly, I read the note. The man who had brought the tea was standing at the front of the restaurant. I could feel his eyes on me. The other customers had gone and now there were only the two of us.

Giving a slight nod of my head, I rose and left. Once outside I turned right, in the direction away from the hospital. I kept on this way for a quarter of a mile, then turned down an alleyway that led between the mud walls of houses. The way twisted and turned. Twice I had to stop because I lost my way. I was not certain that I had read the directions correctly, but continued on. Finally I came to a gate with a faded red star above it. I knocked and waited. Nothing happened and I knocked again. The door opened a crack and I could see an eye. I passed the note and the gate was shut. Several minutes passed; then the gate was opened a few feet and I squeezed through.

A Han with a blotchy complexion and shifty eyes stood before me. He motioned to me to follow him, and we went into the house.

The room we entered was filled with sacks of rice spread about on the floor. On one side there were great wicker baskets filled with onions and garlic. In another corner were tins of oil and spices. There were even two great barrels filled with bean curd floating in oil. An entire side of the room—one complete wall—was obscured by row after row of cans, stacked one atop the other. The labels indicated that they contained preserved meats and fruits.

I pointed to the cans, and the man began to remove some from the stacks. He held up one containing meat, and I said I wanted five more of fruit. I wanted to take some rice and onions but did not know how I would be able to cook the rice. I did not think I could give it to the people in the hospital to cook for Xiyou. Acquiring food illegally was a serious crime, and there could be trouble if I tried that. In the end, I settled on a dozen onions and several strings of garlic.

The man took these, together with the cans, and placed them in a large basket. Then he covered everything with a cloth. When he had finished he turned toward me and said the price would be a hundred yuan. I peeled off the bills, handed them to him, and hoisted the basket to my shoulder. Then we stood facing each other.

I knew where the doorway was and could have gone

out, but I was reluctant to turn my back to the man. He had seen my money.

Finally he smiled—it was a weird, crooked smile—and walked toward the doorway, and I followed him. When he opened the gate for me, he stepped out and looked both ways, then beckoned. I stepped out and he slid back inside, and I heard the bolt snap into place.

I turned and walked quickly back toward the main street. This time I remembered the way and did not get lost. Several times I thought I heard footsteps behind me and stopped, but each time I looked around, the alley was empty. I could see the main street ahead now and walked faster. I had almost reached it when someone struck me from behind.

How many there were I never knew. At the time I thought there were a half-dozen, but later when I thought about it I guessed that the number had been less. Probably only three or four at the most. They were not strong and that was what saved me. I guess they had been weakened by hunger.

The first blow had been aimed at my skull, but instinct must have warned me, for I moved to the side and it crashed into my shoulder. I staggered and dropped the basket, at the same time moving into a crouch with fists cocked.

A man leaped at me, and I struck him in midair with a hard right and he fell in a heap. Another came at me and I kicked him hard in the groin. Then two leaped on me from behind. I flipped one over my shoulder; there was an audible crack when he landed. The other held on, with his hands clasped around my throat. I kicked backward into his groin and heard him moan; at the same time I grabbed two of his fingers and bent them back sharply. He screamed out and relaxed his grip, and I whirled and kicked him. Then one of the fallen men came at me again. This time he advanced with a knife in his hand, slashing at my face.

I grabbed his arm and twisted it and felt his shoulder snap. Then another came at me, then another. I kicked and punched wildly. Someone cut my arm, but I kept swinging. Then, as suddenly as they had appeared, the attackers were gone, and I was alone, standing with a bleeding arm before an overturned basket of food.

When I arrived at the hospital the bleeding had stopped. It was midafternoon. The hallways were still full of people, and they watched me as I passed. I had replaced the cloth over the basket so that the food was hidden, but I could not shake the feeling that they knew what was in the basket.

When I entered Xiyou's room she was sleeping. I sat and watched her. She looked weak—her face was drawn and the dark circles under her eyes were still visible—but she looked more at peace. I could not tell whether this was because she actually felt better, or because she had given up struggling. The doctor's words about the congestion in her lungs and her irregular heartbeat came back to me.

I must have dozed off, for suddenly I heard someone calling me and struggled back through layers of consciousness. Xiyou was sitting up, with a wry smile on her face.

"You took a very long time to have breakfast," she said. "You must have eaten well."

I nodded. Then she saw my arm.

"You have been injured!" she cried.

"It is nothing," I answered.

Her eyes moved to the basket sitting beside the chair.

"Food," I said. "Today you will have enough to eat so that you can begin to regain your strength."

"I cannot," she said. "I cannot eat food that has been gotten illegally."

"I paid for this food," I said. "I did nothing wrong in buying it. If you do not eat you will remain weak and helpless. You can help no one in such a state. There is food in the city for those who look. There is no crime in that. If I had not bought it, then another would have."

Scorn flashed in her eyes. "If one does it, then another will do it . . . then another and another. Soon things will be as they were before Liberation. There will be corruption and exploitation—people will be starving and begging in the streets for a bowl of rice."

I laughed. "They beg for rice now."

"That is only because of the flood," she said. "No one could have prevented this. But in normal times the Chinese people no longer beg—they have enough food in their bellies."

To argue would have been futile. I did the easier thing, bent, took a can from the basket, and opened it. Then I began to eat pieces of preserved pear. I did it slowly, using my knife to spear each dripping segment. The fruit was sweet, the syrup almost sickeningly so, but I continued to swallow piece after piece. When I had finished half the can I looked toward Xiyou.

She lay with her head on the pillow, eyes closed. Her face was turned away from me.

"Already I can feel my strength returning," I said. "I have five more cans of fruit and five cans of meat. Enough to give me back my strength, enough to make certain that I return to Beijing. I will not die of starvation."

"Your words will not tempt me," she said. "I have known hunger before. I have seen people starve, children crying out because of the pain in their bellies. To eat stolen food is to be part of the same corruption that makes those children hungry. Each piece you swallow is taken from their mouths."

I said nothing. Already I was opening a can of meat. It was pork preserved in tomato sauce. Heated it would have been passable, even good, but I had no way of doing this. Still, it tasted wonderful. Now I could no longer feign indifference. I ate quickly, greedily, as fast as I could without choking. I did not look up until the entire can was empty.

Then I stood, covered the remaining cans in the basket with the cloth, placed the half-full can of pears and the knife on the table beside Xiyou's bed, and sat back in the chair. I was very tired and soon slept.

Chapter Nineteen

It was five when I woke. The can of pears was still on the table beside Xiyou's bed. It looked as full as it had when I had fallen asleep. She was sleeping, but her breathing seemed shallow and fast. I put my hand on her forehead. It was cold. Then I felt her pulse—it was weak and irregular.

It took me almost half an hour to find the doctor. He was in another part of the hospital in the rooms where some of the staff lived. There were two nurses on duty. The first did not want to help me and said that she did not know where the doctor was to be found. The second was more sympathetic. She nodded her head in the right direction.

When he came to the door I could tell he had been sleeping. He rubbed his eyes, blinked at me uncomprehendingly for a minute, then remembered.

I told him the symptoms while he got his bag; then we hurried through the corridor. Fear was spreading through me like a pool of cold water: He would be able to do nothing; she would lapse into a coma and that would be the end.

The doctor took one look at her, felt her pulse, then

took something from his bag and filled a large syringe. A few minutes after the injection, her breathing slowed and a trace of color returned to her face.

"It is glucose," he said to me. "She should be fed intravenously, but we don't have enough. This was almost the last in the hospital."

His eyes found the can of pears, and he looked at me questioningly.

"She will eat nothing," I said. "I have food but she refuses it."

He sighed, then reached over and chaffed her wrists. Finally he slapped her gently on the cheek. Her eyelids fluttered.

"You must waken!" he said. His voice sounded stern and fatherly.

Her eyes shut again, and again he slapped her, this time harder.

"I do not have time to humor you. I am tired. There are many patients. You steal the time and energy that they need."

She struggled and finally managed to open her eyes. There was a faraway, tired look in them—as if she had come back from a place she had not wanted to leave.

"Your friend has brought you food. If you do not eat it you will die. We have almost no food in the hospital. The little we have is needed for the other patients. You do not have the right to refuse this food."

She shook her head from side to side.

"To commit suicide is not a virtuous act. It helps no one. Your duty is to live so that you can help China and the Chinese people. Here"—and he took a piece of pear on the end of the knife and held it to her mouth. She kept her lips pressed together for a moment longer, then opened them, and he put the piece of pear in her mouth.

I watched her chew.

"Swallow!" he said, and she did so. Then he gave her another piece of pear. This time she ate it more quickly.

He stood and handed the knife to me.

"Give her all the fruit in the can but no more now—otherwise she will become sick. In three hours feed her again. Have you anything besides pears?"

I told him about the meat. He nodded and rose to leave. I followed him into the hall and held two cans of meat toward him. He shook his head.

"You will need those," he said. "I can get food. There are only three doctors in this town; the government cannot allow me to die."

"If you don't have any meat your strength will fail," I said.

He took the cans and left me.

When I returned to the room I found Xiyou lying as before. She said nothing, and when I fed her the remainder of the pears she ate sullenly, as if I were wounding her with the food. Then she shut her eyes and slept. Night began to fall. I pushed the basket with the food in it underneath the bed where it was out of sight, and sat back in the chair. I had spent so many hours sleeping in it that it had begun to feel comfortable.

I woke near midnight. It was deathly quiet. The only sound was Xiyou's breathing; it seemed regular, not shallow and hurried as it had been. I walked to the window and held my watch up so I could capture some light from the moon: it was eleven thirty. She had slept for almost seven hours. It was time to waken her and give her some more food. I shook her shoulders gently and her eyes opened. A strange combination of emotions filled them—thankfulness mixed with anger and confusion.

I opened a can of pork and tomatoes and started to feed her.

"I am strong enough to do that myself," she said, and I handed her the can and the knife and watched while she ate. When she finished she handed me the can and twisted so that she could look out the window.

It was a very clear night, and the bright moonlight illuminated the courtyard so that all of the flagstones and the heaps of rubbish were clearly visible. Two rats were eating garbage. They were ugly creatures, almost a foot long. She watched them with a dispassionate curiosity.

"At least the rats eat well in Liuyuan," I said.

She looked at me, smiled cynically, and said, "You will be able to leave here soon. The soldiers will fix the bridge, and the trains will run again. Soon you will be in the Peking Hotel eating in the expensive dining room for foreigners. We have each of us learned something. All experience makes one wiser."

"Did Chairman Mao say that?" I asked.

She looked irritated.

"I could not resist," I said. "I'm afraid I am incorrigible. What would you do with someone like me if I lived in China? Probably I would be in a labor camp."

"No," she said, "if you lived in China you would change. You would struggle and resist at first, but in the end you would come to see things as we do."

"We?"

"The Chinese people," she answered.

"How do you know that I would not become like those who cannot conform?"

"There are few criminals," she said. "And even those are not beyond help. We can retrain them and show them the errors in their subjective thinking. It is a long and difficult process, but it can be done."

From somewhere within the hospital came the sound of voices. We stopped talking and listened. The sound was indistinct and distant, yet it echoed in the silent hallways.

"The doctor is very tired," I said at last. "He has little help and there are many sick and his medicine is almost gone."

"He is corrupt," she said, matter-of-factly, as if she were reading off a prepared sheet for public information.

"Because he made you eat?" I asked.

"His political development is primitive," she said. "He has a narrow vision."

"Probably he would benefit from sessions with experts who would reform his subjective thinking," I said.

"Your bourgeois cynicism no longer upsets me," she replied.

We stared at each other for a moment; her face, illuminated by the flickering candle, looked pale. There were still circles under her eyes, but her expression had changed. She looked stronger, almost defiant. The anger pleased me, and suddenly I realized that when she was angry her face became beautiful.

She must have noticed the change in the current of my thoughts, for suddenly she became embarrassed. Neither of us spoke; then, fumbling for words, I said, "In a few days your strength will return. Then I will return to Beijing, and we will never see each other again."

It was not the right thing to say and I knew it, but the words slipped out and then they were there, said, and there was nothing to be done about it.

"Foreigners are strange," she said after a few moments of awkward silence had passed. "They want to be friends but they don't know how."

I said nothing.

"We have become friends," she said. "Nothing can change that. If you were in Beijing and I were in Urumchi it would still be so. Even when you have returned to the West our friendship will continue."

We were looking at each other now—the awkwardness had passed—and suddenly we both smiled.

Chapter Twenty

Morning came almost before I was asleep. Suddenly I was blinking, and the light beyond the window was dazzling. I looked toward the bed. The light had not reached Xiyou yet and she was still sleeping. There was more color in her face and the circles under her eyes had almost faded. Sleeping, she looked like a girl of fifteen.

I stood, stretched, and decided to walk into the city. It was very early and the streets were still empty. I walked to the center of town. Along the way I passed an old man walking slowly with the aid of a cane. He raised his head and stared at me when I passed.

When I reached the main street I turned to the right and walked toward the station. If news of what was happening in the outside world was to be found anywhere in town it would be here.

The front door of the station was barred, and there seemed to be no one in the compound. I started to walk toward the gate when I noticed something moving in the shadows to the right and peered in that direction. Two people were lying close to the wall: one was an old man, the other a young boy. The boy had a peculiar cast to his features, as if he were demented or simple. Both were very near death, the old man breathing in labored gasps, the boy lying on his back with wide eyes staring upward. They both needed food—if they did not get it they would probably die in a matter of hours—but there was nothing I could do. The boy looked toward me, then reached out his hand. His eyes found mine, and we stared at each other. I knew I should look away—it would do me no good to develop those feelings—but something held me. Was it morbid curiosity? I could not tell.

Then, while I watched, the boy's eyelids fluttered rapidly, and suddenly they froze. His gaze was fixed skyward and I knew he had gone.

Outside the gate the city was coming alive. Men were pushing carts, women, weakened by hunger, walked to market in the hopeless quest for food. Standing frozen before the dead boy, I watched them pass. Soon the old man would die too. Now it could only be a matter of minutes. I wanted to call out to someone for help, but it would have done no good. Everyone in Liuyuan was facing death; no one had food to give. The two before me, one a corpse, the other half dead, were the first of many. People could not be expected to mourn. Nobody even had strength enough to carry the corpses to the graveyard, let alone dig graves in the stony soil. Life was cheap—despite a revolution, things were as they had always been in China.

I returned to the hospital near noon. Xiyou was staring out the window again. Though she looked healthier, there was something sad in her expression, as if she had lost something valuable that could not be replaced—a loved one perhaps, or faith in an ideal. Finally she turned from the window and looked at me. The defiance was gone from her eyes—she looked thoroughly defeated.

"People are starving in the city," she said. "The nurse who brought me tea has told me. There is no food and the government can promise none. The people are going back to their old ways—there is profiteering and hoarding and greed."

There was a rap at the door, and it opened. A nurse was there, holding a thermos of hot water. They no longer brought food, and now when they appeared, each had a hungry look in her eye. I felt uneasy about leaving the food in the room but had not told Xiyou this.

I took the thermos, but the nurse remained at the doorway. I watched her as her eyes flitted around the room, searching for the food. They stopped where I knew they would—the place beneath the bed where I had placed the dwindling cans of meat and pears. There were now three cans of meat and two of pears. We had eaten the garlic and the onions.

The woman's eyes were filled with a cold, feral hunger that was frightening. I had seen that look before—it filled the eyes of the people in the street, those who still had strength enough to struggle. It was a light that burned, a glowing fire that was struggling against all the forces of the world that wanted to snuff it out. It had one purpose—to find sustenance—and the means was not important. The first time I had ever seen it was when I was a boy on a vacation in northern Michigan. One day I had come to a place where a farmer had set a trap to catch the foxes who were raiding his chicken coop. A fox had been snared, one of its rear legs caught in the fanged metal jaws of the trap. It had been there for two or three days already without food or water.

When I came on it, it was lying stretched out, resting; probably it was almost too weak to stand. But when I approached, its ears pricked up and its eyes glowed. I moved too near and it was on me in a flash—a tiny animal filled with more fury than I had ever known existed in the world.

The wounds on my legs and arms required over fifty stitches. And worse were the rabies shots the doctor, a clumsy country practitioner, insisted on giving me.

Xiyou coughed and I turned. She looked uneasy, and I asked her what was wrong. She shook her head as if to say it was nothing, and I returned my attention to the nurse, but she had gone, leaving the door open behind her.

I breathed a sigh of relief and shut the door and came to the bed. Xiyou looked frightened. She had felt the woman's hunger more intensely than I had. I could feel her trembling.

"We will go," I said. "It's not safe here. We will take the food and go to my room. There we will wait."

She did not answer, but it did not matter. She was beyond agreeing or disagreeing and would come like a helpless child.

We left the hospital at midnight. Our footsteps echoed for a moment in the empty hallway; then we were passing through the vaulted corridor that led to the street. There were people sleeping here—sick and dying—who had come from the countryside seeking food that was not to be found.

Then we were in the street and turned and headed toward my hotel. We walked quickly, and as we went I glanced from side to side and over my shoulder. I carried a sack with five cans in it, and they contained life for us. The night was filled with people whom hunger had driven into a state where all rules and laws were so much sand in the wind.

Once we passed close to a wall where there were a half-dozen figures huddled. Two rose to follow us. And now, ahead, I could see that figures lay spread on the ground in clumps here and there, like piles of garbage. They were people waiting to die, each filled with a ravening hunger. They could not know that we had food, but they could see us and they could see the sack. We had become prey, for behind us now were a dozen men, moving through the night like a pack of hunger-crazed wolves.

My room was still far away, and even if it had been close it could not have saved us if those following saw us enter. We had to lose them in the night or we were doomed. I thought of dropping the sack—that was what they wanted—but pushed the idea from my mind. That was a last resort. If we had no food we would die.

Ahead was a place where an alley turned off the main street, heading back into a maze of twisted byways that spread like a net through the low, mud-walled houses of the town. I tightened my grip on Xiyou's arm and urged her into a trot.

The alleyway was dark and filled with shadows cast by the moonlight. We moved quickly; Xiyou faltered, and I grasped her arm and pulled her along. We took a turn onto another byway, then turned off on yet another. Still there was the pad of footsteps moving behind us. How many there were I could not tell: perhaps a dozen, possibly more.

Now they sounded closer. It seemed impossible. We had taken a half-dozen turns and were moving faster than we had on the main street, yet they were gaining.

Xiyou was gasping now, struggling valiantly to keep up with me. She could not go on much longer.

Suddenly we came to an open space. Two streets crossed

here. Beyond, the streets widened, and I could see dark shapes lying about. Any way we went, we would have to pass them and they would follow. I grabbed Xiyou and led her close to the wall of one of the houses, and we lay down with the sack between us and covered our faces with our hands.

A few minutes passed. My heart was racing. It was a gamble, but the only chance. Then the sounds of footsteps grew louder, and suddenly the men following entered the intersection and stopped. Before them lay three wide roads, each filled with hundreds of dark shapes, some alive, some dead, some near death. If they had been rational they might have hunted for us, but starving men are not rational. They split into three groups and each hurried off up the road. I listened to their footsteps grow fainter, then pressed Xiyou's arm, and we rose and walked slowly toward the street that we had entered the square on. No one followed us, and once we were beyond the open space we went faster, moving at a quick trot. Somewhere Xiyou had found strength. The moon was overhead, shining down like a great white-faced father. He seemed to be smiling at us.

CHAPTER TWENTY-ONE

By the time we reached the building where I had been staying, the air had turned colder and a strong breeze was blowing. We were both shivering violently. We were soaked with perspiration, and this made matters worse.

The door of the building did not fit tightly and the breeze entered the room. There was no stove and the blanket was thin. We lay on the bed, huddled together for warmth, and tried to sleep. Xiyou shivered violently. The wind seemed to grow stronger minute by minute. I still had strength enough to keep out some of the cold, but she had none, and I began to worry. I tried to cover her with my body and finally held her close, and gradually we began to grow warmer. How long we lay shivering before we fell asleep I do not know. I heard a cock crow somewhere in the city—I remember the sound distinctly because it struck me as incongruous that an animal should be alive when so many people were starving.

I woke first and crawled quietly from the bed and went outside. The sky was blue and cloudless and the breeze had died, but it was bitterly cold. I could tell from the position of the sun that it was midmorning, but there was not a single moving figure in sight. About fifty yards down the road two people lay huddled before a wall. They looked dead. Two vultures were flying overhead, wheeling in circles. I was terribly thirsty and began to search for water.

Two hundred yards down the street, where it crossed with another and broader street, stood a lone water pump. It was coated with ice, and around it the ground was frozen into a sheet of dirty ice. I worked the handle but only a trickle of water came out.

Xiyou was awake when I got back to the room. She looked rested and stronger than I had seen her look in weeks. We ate half a tin of pears and a few pieces of meat each.

When we finished eating we went outside. It was icy cold, but there was no breeze, so it was bearable. I suggested that we go to the center of town to see if there was any news concerning relief. We went back into the room, hid the food beneath some chunks of coal, then went out.

The scene in the middle of town was bizarre. There were hundreds of people standing, sitting, moving about. A policeman in a blue and red uniform stood on the raised platform used to direct traffic. There were no automobiles or trucks moving, but he turned first one way, then the other, pointed to men, told this one to move along, that one to stop. No one paid him the slightest heed.

I went to him and asked if there was word from Urumchi. He continued to direct the invisible trucks and cars and did not reply. Finally I shouted and his trance snapped, and I repeated the question.

A weird, ghoulish grin curled his mouth; then he began laughing hysterically.

I decided to go to the hospital, thinking the doctor might have some news.

"We'll only stop for a few minutes," I said. "Then we will go back to the new room by another route. The nurse will not be able to follow."

I could tell that she wasn't convinced.

It took me almost half an hour to find the doctor. The hospital itself was almost empty, but outside its walls and in the vaulted archway that led to the main courtyard lay hundreds of dying people. The doctor was in his room, lying on the bed, smoking.

He gave me a weary smile when I entered. "You were wise to leave. The next day the nurses left, taking all the food that remained with them. No, no, don't worry!" he said, anticipating my question. "I continue to eat. Each day a jeep appears three times and each time I am ridden to the mess hall on the north side of the town where the army officers stay. They feed me rice and salt pork, and that is enough to keep me alive."

"Is there word from Urumchi or Beijing?" I asked.

He shook his head.

"Then there is no prospect of food?"

"None," he said. "It is four weeks since the flood and still they do not come. A man could walk from Urumchi to here with a basket of rice in that time. They could send camels and mules overland, even drop supplies from the air. But . . ."

He shrugged.

I could feel Xiyou's presence near me. She had heard the doctor's words, and I could imagine her thoughts. I had not wanted her to go through this—she had suffered enough and was just regaining her strength. The truth could be devastating.

"It is not as you say!" she said, and the clarity and strength of her voice amazed me. "The way from Urumchi is far. There are mountains and deserts to cross. No man can travel that route alone. In the old days, before we had the train, it sometimes took months for a caravan to cross the desert."

I watched the doctor's face. I could see a retort rise to his lips, but then he decided against it and merely shrugged and inhaled on his cigarette.

"Is there any word in the newspaper or on the radio?" I asked.

"They speak of it on the radio," he said with a cynical smile. " 'There is some difficulty in Xinjiang because of the recent floods, but the people are adjusting well. The local leaders have assured the government in Beijing that things will soon be back to normal.' Those are the words they use."

Xiyou tugged on my arm. "We learn nothing here," she said.

"Go, my friends," said the doctor, waving the hand holding his cigarette toward the door. "Go back to the city of the dead and dying. Wish them well for me."

We walked down the corridor. Both were silent. We passed the people who filled the vaulted archway. They were countless now. Before, there had been perhaps fifty or sixty; now their number was two or three hundred at least. They did not speak, and most had the wide, staring eyes of those near death.

When we reached the street we turned west, heading toward our room. We had gone about a quarter of a mile when I changed my mind. I had been thinking about our food. We had only one and a half cans of pears and half a can of meat left. That would last perhaps four days, and we would be weaker each day. I had hoped the doctor could give us news of relief, but what he had told us only increased my worries. We needed more food, and I thought I knew where we could find it.

It took almost three hours to work our way through the maze of streets to the gate of the house. I knocked. Several minutes passed. I knocked again. Finally there were footsteps and I could feel ourselves being scrutinized. I took a fifty-yuan bill from my pocket and held it so it could be seen clearly by whoever was on the other side of the gate. There was a grunt and the bar was removed and the gate opened a few feet and we slid through.

The man looked as before. His complexion was as blotched, his eyes as shifty. He led us to the house and we went inside. I heard Xiyou gasp.

There were not so many cans as before—only half the wall was covered—but there were more vegetables, and sack upon sack of rice stacked from floor to ceiling, filling over a third of the room.

The man was watching Xiyou, an ugly, half-formed smile on his face. I pointed to the cans and held up both hands with all the fingers extended. He took ten cans of meat from the stack. I pointed to the fruit. Some were cans of pears, others of oranges. Finally I took some vegetables and a sack of rice. He took out an abacus and began to calculate.

The lot came to 500 yuan. That meant the rate had more than doubled. It figured—he was a good capitalist: the demand dictated the price. I took out the money and paid him, and he filled a basket, covered it with a cloth, then went and stood by the door. I lifted the basket to my shoulder—I had to struggle to do this—then he smiled a yellow-toothed smile and opened the door and led the way out.

We had walked nearly halfway back to our room before either spoke. I broke the silence.

"If we do not eat we will die. That man is an evil thing, worse than a snake, but there is no other way."

She said nothing.

"He buys from the peasants," I said. "Even now there is food and people who buy and sell it. It is wrong, but it is the way of life."

She cleared her throat and spat. It was the first time I had ever seen her do this. Chinese spit constantly, but she had never done so in my presence before.

We passed an entire family huddled in the recess of a wall: a mother and father, probably middle aged, though it was impossible to tell age with people so near death, and four children. The oldest was perhaps ten, the youngest not more than a year or so. The children were stretched out, staring at the sky. When we passed, the youngest child moaned.

I felt Xiyou flinch; then she stopped. She would not go farther and I knew that nothing would make her move from that place. Her eyes were fixed on mine, and there was no answer I could give that stare.

"Only two cans," I said feebly. "And not all of the rice."

But it did not matter what I said and I knew it.

Chapter Twenty-Two

We returned to the room quickly. The basket was lighter and we walked fast. There were now five cans of fruit and four of meat. We had a half-dozen handfuls of rice wrapped in a piece of cloth and a half-dozen onions. We had given over half the food to the family. It was sheer folly. They were too far gone for it to make any difference. They would die and the food would be taken by others who would die.

We had finished the can of meat we had left behind, ate an onion apiece, then a few pieces of pear. "We will save the rice," Xiyou said. "When we need it we can start a fire and I will cook it."

I nodded dumbly. I thought it best to let her plan—it gave her the feeling that she was in control of things, and she needed that. That was an illusion, of course—she probably sensed this—but she clung to it so fiercely I thought it better not to dislodge it. I had enough money so that we could buy more food if need be. The important thing was to stay alive, to live day by day and not do anything foolish. If we could only hang on, something would change.

As the sun died the cold increased. We pulled the blanket

tightly around ourselves and sat hunched over, grasping our knees. But even this did no good. Then the wind began to howl. It rattled the door and surged around the edges and along the floor, each gust chilling us to the bone.

I decided that we had to build a fire; otherwise we might catch pneumonia. But I had no matches and no idea where I could get any. And even matches would not be enough. We needed kindling wood, and I had seen none of this in the city. My eyes fell on the basket we had carried the food in. It would burn. We could burn the cloth and use this as tinder to ignite the basket. From this we might generate enough heat to light the coal.

Matches were the immediate problem. Without them I could not start a fire, and to find some in the city at night would be impossible. Then I remembered my boy scout days, rose, and in the darkness broke the basket into pieces, picked out two, and began rubbing them together.

It took nearly twenty minutes, but finally I generated enough heat and the cloth began to smolder. But a sudden gust of wind blew it out. The second time I tried, it was quicker. The cloth smoldered and then burst into flame. There was a cheer behind me and then Xiyou was at my side, on her hands and knees, rubbing two chunks of coal together to form a fine powder. This flamed up instantly. She continued to do this, and I did the same. Then, gradually, we added larger and larger pieces of coal until several large chunks were glowing. I used a small shovel I found in the corner of the room to place the coals in the stove. We added more pieces and soon we had a real fire.

We crouched by the stove and warmed our hands.

"Foreigners do not know how to build fires," Xiyou said as she rubbed her arms and shoulders.

"The fire is burning, isn't it?" I said.
"It would never have burned if I hadn't showed you how," she said. There was humor in her voice, but I chose to ignore it.
"You should have shown me how earlier," I replied. "Then we would not have had to freeze through half the night."
"I thought the lesson would be good for you," she said. "I wanted you to feel what a peasant feels."
I gave her a shove and she toppled over. Then we both broke into laughter. She lay on the floor, laughing happily, her face glowing in the firelight. We were warm. We had food to last a few days. It seemed almost too good to be true.

While we slept, the wind grew in volume. It was late in the night when I woke to add coal to the fire. Now the wind seemed to be roaring. The air that entered around the door's edges was frigid, filled with a fine powder, half dust, half snow.
I finished adding coal to the stove, poked the glowing coals with the shovel, then got back into bed.
Xiyou stirred, then rolled over. Her face was lit by the glow from the stove. There was a scar over one eye and pockmarks on her cheeks. It was a peasant's face, not beautiful, but strong and full of character.
Her eyelids fluttered, and I knew she was dreaming. I wondered what those dreams were. Of her mother and father? of suffering? of the glorious promises of the Party?
Suddenly the door rattled louder and flew open, a great gust of wind sweeping into the room. We both leaped up. Choking dust filled the air, and Xiyou started to cough violently. I rushed to the door and, leaning my shoulder

against it, forced it shut. The latch was useless, and I yelled to Xiyou to bring some pieces of coal. These we hammered around the door as wedges. Then we took what was left of the cloth that had covered the food and tried to fill in the cracks to keep the wind out.

When we had finished, the roar of the wind was softer and the room was still. The coal in the stove was glowing—the wind had fanned the fire—and everything was covered with a thick layer of dust. Wearily we went back to the bed and shook out the blanket. I added more coal to the fire and we lay down again.

We were almost asleep when the sound of knocking brought us back to consciousness.

I rose and went to the door and hesitated. I did not know who was on the other side: a starving old woman? a helpless child? perhaps a dozen men, driven to frenzy by hunger? Whoever was outside knew of our presence because of the smoke from the stove, but unless he were strong he would not be able to force the door.

The knocking sounded again, this time fainter. Then there was the sound of scratching, as if a small animal were struggling to get in. I knocked out the pieces of coal I had wedged between the door and its frame and opened it. A young woman was lying on the ground. In her arms was a baby.

They were nearly frozen, and the woman was so weak from hunger that she could not walk. I carried her to the sleeping platform, and laid her down and wrapped her in the blanket. Her eyelids flickered, but she did not speak. Xiyou took the baby and warmed it by the fire. Then she cleaned an old iron pot that lay in the corner of the room and began to boil some rice in it. When this was done she fed it to the child.

The child's face was chapped and its lips cracked, but it ate the food greedily and cried out for more. It looked very weak and worn, but strong enough to survive. The woman was another matter. Probably she had given whatever food she had or could find to her child. How many days she had been without food I could not tell, but she was in a state of semiconsciousness and babbled meaningless sounds. Xiyou tried to feed her some rice, but she could not swallow, and it dribbled from the corner of her mouth. Finally she drank some rice water. That seemed to revive her, and I realized that she was dehydrated and held a cup of water to her lips. She drank this greedily and asked for more. We gave her more rice water and finally she fell asleep.

The storm blew itself out just before dawn, and it became deathly still and biting cold. We added coal to the fire and tried to fill in the cracks around the door so that the heat in the room would not escape.

The woman slept on. Once she woke and called for more water, and we gave it to her and fed her some rice gruel. Then she slept again. Xiyou held the baby in her arms, cooing softly to it and rocking it to and fro. After its first cries for food had been satisfied, it made no further sounds but stared at her in silent fascination.

We opened a tin of meat and another of oranges. Xiyou cooked more rice and we added an onion. Excepting the bowl of rice I'd had in the restaurant near the hospital, it was the first real food, cooked food, I had eaten in weeks, and it tasted unbelievably good.

The woman ate, then slept again. The baby remained silent. Toward nightfall, when Xiyou set it down on the bed for a minute so that she could go outside and relieve herself, it began to cry. I picked it up, and it stared at me with terror-filled eyes. I rocked it gently from side to side; then I held up a finger and the baby reached for it. Its grip was amazingly strong. I wiggled the finger and a flicker of expression—a faint trace of a smile—appeared on his face.

When Xiyou returned she watched us for a minute, then lay down on the bed and shut her eyes. She must have been terribly tired, for she had not recovered her strength yet and had not slept in almost twenty hours. I looked at her and she smiled up at me. Even before the smile had passed from her lips, her eyelids were closing and in a minute she slept too.

I was absolutely still. I listened to the breathing of the woman. It was shallow but steady. The baby lay in her arms, grasping her finger firmly. I tried to move my hand, and the baby squeezed my finger. I looked down, and the baby smiled—this time the smile was distinct and definite.

I wondered what the men in the Agency would have said if they saw me. I had come to Xinjiang to pick up information. God knew what, but it was top secret. The information in the parcel I still carried beneath my shirt would probably make little difference in the long run, but the agency had thought it important enough to send me thousands of miles, across an ocean and deserts, to get it. It was all part of the game, and the men who played it were deadly serious. They did not hold babies and feed starving women; they infiltrated and spied—sometimes they murdered. I had slipped into another role, and it felt strange, but the feeling was not wholly new. When I had once tried to explain it to someone lying in the darkness at my side, I had said that it was like having blunt fingernails. "The feeling is excruciating," I had said. "It is as if I were a declawed cat."

She had laughed at that, because she did not understand.

And I had merely shrugged in the darkness, then began, once again, to go through the motions of love. That frosted over the feeling, buried it. But it did not kill it. One could never kill a feeling. It hunted you out. And now, at last, in a place at the ends of the earth, it had found me again.

Chapter Twenty-Three

In the next few days the weather softened. The sky filled with clouds and sometimes the sun was obscured, but the air turned warmer and there was no breeze.

The woman had regained some strength. She still slept most of the time, but after her midday meal she managed to stay awake for a few minutes and speak to Xiyou. I sat on the platform, watching them. The baby lay on its back, smiling at its mother. Xiyou was beside the mother, feeding her gruel. They looked comfortable, and their faces were filled with the relief that food and sleep give after a long struggle to stay alive.

Then the woman slept again, and Xiyou played with the baby for a while, rocking and tickling it. It smiled once and made a sound that was almost a chuckle. It was amazing the difference that only a few days of food and warmth had made in the baby's appearance. It might have been a healthy, happy child who had enjoyed safety and comfort all of its days. It would take longer for the mother to recover.

"The woman cannot understand what has happened," Xiyou said. "Before, there was always food. Her parents told her stories of the past when this was not so, but she thought that those times would never return. She thinks that the leaders have failed the people—that they are corrupt. She says that she was always told that the Russians and the capitalists were villains, but now she knows that Chinese men can also be evil."

I watched Xiyou's eyes. They were filled with the blank expression of someone who does not want to think about the implications of what she says.

" She is weak and still frightened," I said at last. "When her strength returns she'll feel more optimistic. She still feels death all around her, and this makes her bitter and pessimistic."

But Xiyou did not seem to have heard. She was at the stove, removing the pot containing the rice so that it would not burn. Then she began to sweep the floor. I went outside.

The sky was overcast and the air filled with a thick mist. No one was in sight. I could see the two corpses lying before the wall fifty yards down the road. They lay as they had lain a half-dozen days before. Even with the cold they would have begun to rot, and now, with the warmer air, the process would go faster. Soon the town would be filled with the smell of rotting flesh. Then there would be disease. Most would be near death by then, so it would make little difference; perhaps to many it would be welcome, for it would finish the job more quickly.

I had spent too many days cooped up in the room and was restless. I felt guilty about leaving Xiyou and the woman and child alone, but decided that I could risk a few hours away, so I returned to the room and told Xiyou I was going into the center of town again.

The streets were quieter. They were littered with bodies, now mostly still. Few had the strength to walk. The policeman who had been directing traffic in the center of town was gone. Before the hospital were hundreds of people, all near death. I threaded my way through the people who filled the vaulted archway and entered the building. It was as quiet as a tomb.

The door to the doctor's room was shut. I knocked but there was no answer, so I started to leave. Then, on impulse, I turned the knob and stepped in.

The smell was horrible. He lay on the bed, his head to one side, his chin and chest covered with a skin of dried vomit mixed with blood. How long he had been dead I could not tell, but in the room, shielded by walls from the freezing winds, the body had decayed fast. The stomach was bloated and the face puffy, the eyes bulging. On the small table beside him was a half-empty jar that probably had contained the poison he had taken.

I left quickly. The sky had cleared and the sun, sinking in the west, was a golden ball of fire on the horizon. The quiet was profound. Overhead wheeled a flock of birds. They circled quickly, hovered, flew on.

Xiyou was preparing the evening meal by the time I returned. The woman was lying on her side on the sleeping platform, playing with her child. She tickled it, then lifted it up, and it laughed with pleasure. The fire in the stove had warmed the room, and I began to feel drowsy. We ate rice and onions. Each had two pieces of pear.

Xiyou opened the door of the stove and the room was bathed in a soft, golden light. Soon the baby and the woman were sleeping. Xiyou asked what I had seen in the town and I said, "Many corpses and the doctor—also a corpse."

She did not reply, but went to the far corner of the platform and lay down with her face to the wall.

"What will happen to us?" she said.

"Nothing," I replied. "We will wait until men come with food. They must come sooner or later. We will not starve while I have money, and I still have much."

She was silent. Soon I heard the sound of her breathing deepen and knew that she was sleeping.

I watched the fire slowly die. When it had almost gone out, I rose and added some more coal, poking the embers until they flamed up again. I was becoming an expert at tending fires—now I could make a lone piece of coal last for nearly half a day.

Briefly the wind rose, then died down again. I wanted to sleep but it would not come. The restlessness I had felt in the morning had not gone. My walk in the city had stilled it temporarily, but now it was returning, and when I shut my eyes the face of the doctor appeared, distorted and swollen hideously. I tried to think of something to drive the vision away, to squelch the feeling of death that was overwhelming me, but nothing worked.

The wind began to rise again, pelting the house with a fine spray of sand. Gradually I grew drowsy; then I heard the sound of footsteps outside, not a single pair but several. They stopped, then started again. Several people were approaching the house, moving stealthily, probably drawn by the smell of smoke from the stove. Before I could rise, the door had burst open and a half-dozen men rushed in.

Their faces were worn and reddened by the wind and they were gaunt, but they possessed the strength of desperation. I swung out and knocked one to the ground, but two were on me. Xiyou had leaped at another, slashing at his face with her nails. He flung her aside as if she were a piece of paper. Then they were all on me, pummeling me and trying to hold me down. I struggled for a few minutes more, then relaxed and let them hold me.

While three pinned me to the ground, the others took the food; then they were gone into the night.

I stood up, panting. I had a few cuts and bruises but nothing serious. Xiyou was shaking in terror, and the woman was cowering in the corner of the sleeping platform, hunched over the child.

I shut the door; then we all sat on the sleeping platform, trying to calm ourselves. The baby had begun to cry.

A sudden gust of wind blew the door open again and Xiyou gave a cry like a frightened animal and clung to me. From somewhere outside, we heard shouts and curses.

"They are fighting over the food they have stolen," I said.

Xiyou's shoulders were shaking with silent sobs.

"Tomorrow we must find another place to stay," I said. "They know where we are and they know that we have food. They will return."

The woman looked at me with a blank expression. Her face was pale, but she did not seem to have been affected as Xiyou had. She picked up her child and started rocking it to and fro, humming softly as she did so.

Early the next morning we left the room. It had become warmer and the wind had died. The woman was still weak but she could walk. Xiyou carried the child. I did not know which way we should go, but knew that we had to move at least a few miles away. When the men came again they would look for smoke. We could try to live without heat, but with the child it would be difficult. There would be many buildings empty—or, if not empty, filled with corpses.

We took a narrow twisting alleyway that wove between high walls, entered a square, then passed into another alleyway. Still we had not seen a single person. I searched the sky for smoke—a sign of life—but there was none. Xiyou walked close to me. The attack had shaken her deeply. The woman walked unsteadily, and sometimes I had to support her.

We entered a long, narrow street. Near the end was an abandoned cart. I pushed this to a gate, then climbed onto it. Standing on the cart and extending my arms, I was still three feet from the top of the wall. I leaped and got one hand over the edge, pulled, managed to get the other over, then painfully pulled myself up.

From the top of the wall I peered into the courtyard but could see nothing. I lowered myself, then leaped. Immediately there were high-pitched squeaks and squeals—the sound of rats scurrying. I went to the gate and told Xiyou to move away, and opened it.

Scores of rats flooded past me, squeaking and squealing as they went. I told the woman to wait and went back into the house.

What was left of the inhabitants lay in the main room. All four of them had been reduced to bone. They lay face up, grinning hideously in the bright morning light. I went back to the courtyard, took a large basket, and returned to the main room and threw the bones into it. I covered them with the ashes that remained in the stove and carried the basket out into the courtyard and put it in the far corner, behind a compost pile. Then I told Xiyou and the woman to come in.

The house had four rooms: a large main room, a kitchen, and two storerooms. The sleeping platform occupied one end of the main room. It was large enough for a half-dozen people. There was enough coal to last for weeks, if need be, and a box of matches to make starting a fire easy work.

I went to the courtyard and stepped cautiously out into the street and looked both ways. Still there was no one in sight, but there was no telling when a wandering band of scavengers might appear. Smoke was a signal, a beacon, for the sky was absolutely clear and smoke could be seen from far off. We would have to do without fire. I had not thought it possible, for the room we had been living in was unbearably cold, but this house had thicker walls, and the main room was situated so that it would be exposed to the sun's rays for most of the afternoon. It would not be comfortable without a fire, but we would survive. We could eat our food without cooking it.

I wondered how much longer we would have to wait for relief. The more I thought about our situation, the grimmer it seemed to become. I needed something to occupy my mind or I would panic, so I began to move things in the courtyard, aimlessly rearranging carts and baskets.

In half an hour I had moved everything to a new location and sat down on the edge of a giant clay urn to survey my work. I had worked hard and was sweating, and the parcel beneath my shirt had rubbed the skin raw. I seldom removed it, not even when I slept, but there was no one in sight and the skin had begun to itch, so I pulled the parcel out.

The brown-paper wrapping was damp and torn in several places. Beneath it I could see sheets of paper with figures on them. It suddenly struck me that I should study what was written on those sheets of paper; that way if they were lost or stolen, the mission would not be a total loss.

At first I could make no sense of the sheets. There were a dozen pages, filled with figures, and a few sentences in Chinese. But gradually, as I pored over them, the figures on the sheets began to fall into a pattern. There were two columns: one contained a list of the uranium content of different bombs. It took longer to discover the meaning of the figures in the second column. Finally I realized that they indicated area: probably, I surmised, in square kilometers. The figures in the second column indicated the area devastated by the blast. I knew I was only guessing, but also knew that if I could supply the ratio between the size of the bombs in the first column and the blast areas in the second column, then the men in the home office could fill in the rest of the information. So I set out to analyze the figures and to discover a ratio. After an hour I had found what I wanted. Each time the amount of uranium in the bomb increased by half, the area devastated was doubled, then squared. It was a simple equation, straightforward and unequivocal. It was only if you thought about it that you realized its consequences—the number of men, women, and children who would be blown to smithereens if a bomb of a certain size were dropped in a heavily populated area.

I wrapped the sheets up in the brown paper and placed the parcel beneath my shirt again; then I sat back to consider the significance of what I had read.

The information had been passed to me by a man in Xinjiang. He was a local operator, working for whatever he could make. His contacts had to be local. Probably they originated in Urumchi, which was the administrative center for the region. Xinjiang encompassed untold miles of desert. The population was sparse and centered around a few cities. The region was ideal for the testing of nuclear weapons. Even in Beijing I had heard rumors of tests in the far western sector of the province, near the Russian and Afghan borders. Between that area and the populous cities—Urumchi and Turpan—lay thousands of miles of desert. Any clouds of radioactive dust would probably dissipate long before they drifted to the east. And if they went to the west—well, in that direction lay Russian territory. The Chinese could not be terribly concerned with what happened there. It was obvious then: the figures on the sheets represented the results, some actual, others projected, of nuclear tests conducted in Xinjiang. The agency would be interested in that data. There was a big central office manned by hundreds of taciturn automatons who collected information of that nature and filed it away until one of the men who sat in plush offices called for it. The director of the Agency had access to those files—and through him, the Secretary of Defense and the President. Every time they made a decision involving foreign policy they consulted those files. Idealists preached; liberals complained about the military-industrial complex; politicians bent on making a reputation because of their advocacy of a cause harangued; and all the while the President and his Secretary of State assessed the relative strengths of the different parties in a dispute, made an educated guess about what the future held, and made their policy accordingly. Those decisions were done with a cold, calculated, remorseless sense of national self-interest—and for them, figures such as those contained on the sheets that rested next to my chest, now rubbing the already raw skin even rawer, were considered vital. Christ! I thought. You're an important son of a bitch!

When I went back into the house I found Xiyou and the woman and child sitting on the sleeping platform, staring into space. They said nothing, but I knew what they were thinking. We had no food and the pangs of hunger were beginning to grow.

"Do not light a fire," I said. "Lock the gate behind me.

When I return I will knock three times. Remember: three knocks."

Xiyou rose and followed me to the gate.

"Will you be able to find the place again?" she asked, half reluctantly. She knew that we needed food, but her conscience was troubling her.

"I will find it," I said. "There are four or five hours of light left, and that will be enough time."

I pushed the gate open and waited until she had closed and bolted it before I turned up the street.

It took less than an hour. The gate was the fourth from the end of the street. It looked stronger than the others, as if it had been specially built to protect the goods that lay behind it.

I knocked and waited but no one came. I tried again, pounding the gate until the blows echoed in the empty street. Still there was no response. Then I pushed against it and it swung open easily, and I walked into the courtyard. The blanket that covered the door of the house hung by a corner, as if someone had started to tear it down, and the door itself was open. I stepped to the entrance and waited, listening for a sound from within, but there was only silence. I went in.

The room was bare—not a can or a grain of rice remained. They had found it. I had known it would happen sooner or later; the miracle was that the man had been able to do business, if that was what you could call it, for as long as he had.

I left and began to wander through the city. I knew there was no food to be found, but I did not want to accept the fact. But once in the center of the city I realized the situation was hopeless. Those around me were all starving peasants; there was not an official or soldier in sight. They had all gone somewhere, perhaps to safety, but I doubted that they had left. If anyone had food, they did. Then I remembered the doctor's words about the army camp on the north side of town, and began walking in that direction.

It was situated almost a mile beyond the edge of the town. A road twisted and turned, snaking its way across the gravel and rock desert. There were four buildings, all built of red brick and all covered with roofs of rusted, corrugated tin. A jeep and a broken-down bus were parked on one side of a lot.

From a quarter of a mile away the buildings looked uninhabited, but when I got closer I noticed fresh tire tracks in the dust of the roadway. Then I saw a thin wisp of smoke rising from a pipe that came out of one of the buildings.

I knocked, but no one came to the door. I tried again, this time knocking much harder. The result was the same. I heard shouts and grumbles from within, the kind of sounds drunken men make when they are no longer coherent. I tried to push the door open, but it would not yield, so I walked to the side of the building and peered in through the dirty windows.

A dozen men lay sprawled about, some on the floor, others in chairs. I could see bottles sitting on tables. Some of the men were still drinking; others had collapsed, apparently having drunk themselves into a stupor. I could have pounded on the door forever and it would have done no good.

I had already turned back down the roadway and walked a few hundred feet when it occurred to me that I should check the other buildings. There might be sober men in them, and it was certain that somewhere there was a

shortwave radio. No base would be totally isolated from the rest of the People's Liberation Army.
 The building nearest the roadway seemed completely empty. There was no window, and pounding on the door brought no one. The door itself seemed solid—the kind of door you would place on a storeroom. If there was food, it was in this building. I marked it in my mind, then went to the next.
 This was a large building with numerous windows on each side. The windows had been covered from the inside with pieces of cardboard, so I could see nothing. I rapped on the door and heard what I thought was an answering shout from within. So I pushed it open.
 The building was lined with row after row of bunk beds, stretching from floor to ceiling. It was dark. The only light was the flickering flame of a kerosene lantern. I squinted into the darkness but could see no one. From somewhere far within came a greeting.
 "You—at the door! You, foreigner!"
 I moved toward the direction of the sound. A man was lying on a bunk completely in shadow. I could see only the bottoms of his feet, which were sticking out from beneath a blanket.
 When I got closer he sat up and stared at me. He looked like a boy in his early twenties. He needed a shave but otherwise appeared healthy.
 "I came from the city," I said. "I am seeking news of the outside. When will relief come? When will the trains run again?"
 He continued to stare at me, as if dumbfounded, and I repeated the questions.
 "Where are you from, foreigner?" he asked. "How have you come to this place?"

"I am a Canadian," I said, "and how I have come to this place is a story too long to tell. Where is your radio? I must make a call to my embassy."

"The radio is in the building near the dining hall," he said. "But only Wang Gui-lin can operate it and he is in the dining hall."

"And he is drunk," I answered.

The soldier nodded. "Yes, he is drunk like all of the others. What else would you have them do, foreigner? All day they bury the dead. They need something to wash the taste of death from their mouths."

"When will the government send relief?" I said. "How long must the people in the town wait?"

He shrugged and said he didn't know.

"Do you hear nothing from the authorities in Urumchi?" I asked. "Surely they must contact you sometime."

"Only Wang Gui-lin knows that," he said, then lay down again.

I left and started for the mess hall, then stopped. If Wang Gui-lin was in there, he was too drunk to help me. I would waste time and probably put myself in a dangerous position: there was no telling how drunken men would react to an outsider.

Those thoughts were going through my head when the door of the mess hall opened and a man stepped out. He was about forty-five or fifty and walked with an erect, steady bearing, as though completely sober. When he saw me he stopped and greeted me.

"I have come from the city," I said. "I seek news."

"There is none to be had," he said.

"The soldier in the barracks told me Wang Gui-lin is the radio operator. He must know something," I said.

"Wang Gui-lin is drunk," said the man. "Like the

others, he drinks until he falls senseless. You will waste your time on him."

"Do you know anything?" I asked. "Is there no news from Urumchi?"

"They tell us to wait," he said. "They say a relief caravan is on its way—trucks crossing the desert—but that the road has been washed away and the journey is difficult."

"When did they say this? When is the caravan to arrive?" I asked.

"The last communication from Urumchi came a week ago," he said. "The caravan set out ten days before that."

"But the distance is only seven hundred fifty kilometers," I said. "Surely they should have arrived by now."

"Do you see them?" said the man. "If they were here you would know it. We would not hide them. Do you think these men enjoy burying the dead each day?"

I turned and began to walk back to the town, and the man called after me.

"Do not speak to the others about us. We do not have food for them."

It was after dark when I returned to the house. I knocked three times and the door opened. Xiyou tried to hide the expression in her eyes when I told her of the food that was not to be found. The woman listened, lying on her side with her eyes fixed on me. Her face registered no emotion: it was as if she had expected the answer I brought. She had been through so much that she had forgotten how to be disappointed. Everything that happened was a fact—she seemed to regard the world as something about which it was futile to hope or despair.

That night I slept uneasily. Twice I awakened and listened to the breathing of the others. The woman and child's was regular and deep, but from Xiyou's side of the bed came only the sound of normal breathing. She was not sleeping. It could not be hunger, for it was not yet intense enough to cause sleeplessness. Something else was gnawing at her, but she said nothing, and in the morning appeared as always: quietly accepting whatever fate the gods or the leaders bequeathed to her.

As the day wore on I grew more and more restless. I could feel my strength ebbing, and knew that in a few days I would barely be strong enough to walk. Hunger worked that quickly on a healthy man who had been eating regularly, and it had been over a month since I had eaten regularly.

By early afternoon I had decided. The town was filled with rats—we would have to eat them. I had seen others doing this but never joined them. Now we had no choice. Xiyou watched me mutely, and when I went to the gate carrying the sack and iron rod, she followed me. "Three knocks as before," I said as I stepped into the alleyway. She nodded and then the gate swung shut and I heard the bar drop into the brackets.

I walked quickly, peering up each street and alley I passed. They were all empty, and I began to wonder whether I had waited too long to begin my hunt.

Finally, when I had almost reached the center of town, I began to encounter groups of people. I approached four women and a child and watched them. They were crouched low, squatting, and they ate steadily. One of the women had a knife. With this she cut away chunks of flesh from the corpses of fat gray rats, and the others grabbed these.

What my next move would be I didn't really know. I

knew that I needed meat but I didn't want to join the group. I wouldn't be able to eat it raw. For some reason I had convinced myself that if only it were cooked it would be different. We would roast the meat over the fire in the courtyard. That way at least the house would not be filled with the smell.

I left the center of town and began to walk southwest. I had never gone in this direction before, and the streets seemed wider, the houses larger and more prosperous-looking. I had gone about a mile in this direction when I stopped. There had been no rats and it was becoming apparent that if I were to find some I would have to return to the center of town.

Then, suddenly, I spotted a human corpse. It lay in a gate, half in the roadway, half inside a courtyard, as if the person had been trying to leave his house when he died. Around it were a dozen rats, fat ugly creatures, feeding like vultures. I crouched and approached slowly; the rats saw me but didn't leave their feast. A few reared up on their hind legs and peered at me.

I began to wield the iron rod, battering the rats. They squealed and fled. Four lay behind, still twitching. These I continued to pound until all movement had stopped. Then I put the bodies in my sack and moved on. By late afternoon the sack was filled, and I returned to the house.

I rapped three times and Xiyou opened the gate. Her eyes fixed themselves on the bloody sack.

"We will build a fire," I said. "That way the flavor will not be so rank. Otherwise we will sicken and lose the nourishment."

She nodded and began to put small pieces of coal in the fireplace. There was something mechanical in her movements, as if she were under a spell. When she had finished, we tried to start the fire. It took several minutes because we kept dropping the matches; then, when the paper lighted, the wood would not catch. Finally, though, the coals were glowing, and we skinned the carcasses and placed them on the blackened bars that formed a grill above the fire.

Immediately the meat sizzled and turned brown. We watched the blood ooze out of the flesh and drip into the flames; the flesh began to turn brown and crisp. We waited a few more minutes then used a knife to lift it from the fire and placed it on a platter Xiyou had found in a corner of the main room.

We went inside then and began to eat. Nobody spoke and we did not look at each other. We ate steadily, our heads bowed. With the first bite I expected revulsion, perhaps nausea. Instead there was only a strange feeling, as if I were rising off the earth, floating out to a place I had never been and from where I could watch another man who looked amazingly like me eat strips of grilled rat meat.

When we finished we moved apart. Xiyou sat in the corner, staring listlessly ahead into space. The woman retreated to the sleeping platform, where she shut her eyes. The baby curled up beside her, sleeping contentedly. I had watched her tear off strips of the flesh, chew them to make them more tender, then place them in his mouth. The baby had accepted them with a gurgle of content that made me feel nausea.

So the days passed, and with their passing, spring approached and the air warmed and there were more clouds, white puffs high on the horizon, and then the wind began to blow and dust was everywhere—in the streets, in the courtyard, surging around the edges of the door and windows. It was a fine yellow powder, finer than talcum, and it covered our faces and our hands and filled our nostrils. We coughed and spat but could not clear our throats, and all night the child whined.

I became frightened that his cries would draw marauders to us, so I plugged the spaces around the door tightly with cloth to deaden the sound and help keep out the dust. Perhaps the wadding did the former, for we were left alone almost until the end, and then it was not the baby's cries that brought them. But somehow the dust entered anyway, and in the mornings the table, which had been wiped clean at night, was always covered with a layer of yellow powder.

"It is the way of Gansu," Xiyou said. "The wind never stops blowing in the spring, and the dust comes down from Mongolia and from the desert in Xinjiang."

I thought of the land out there, beyond the edge of town. That was a hard land to cross in the best of times, in the winter when one had only the cold to fight or in the late autumn when it rained. But now, with the dust, it would be impossible. And so I gave up hoping for the relief column from Urumchi.

▽

Chapter Twenty-Four

One day the dust finally began to let up. It did not stop altogether, but it was thinner so that I could walk in the courtyard without having to shield my eyes or wear a piece of cloth over my mouth and nose. I had been in the house for untold days and I was restless. Worse, our supply of rat meat was low—we had only two pieces, grilled and dried long ago. I took my knife and the bloodstained sack and told Xiyou to bar the gate behind me. Each time I had gone out I repeated the same warning, that the child must be kept quiet and that they should not start a fire or go for water. During the days of the wind we had sometimes burned a fire, but that had been only at night when the smoke was not visible and the wind so strong and persistent that it scattered the smoke, so that no one could have found the house by following the smell. Now I said these same things again, adding that I would knock three times as I had always done before when I wanted to re-enter. "Remember," I said, "three times only. If you do not come I will wait after that—at least a full minute—and then give three more knocks."

To all of this she nodded mutely, and then I went out,

waited until I heard the bar dropped back into the brackets, then turned and headed up the street.

The city seemed nearly deserted, and worse, the rats were so few and so small that they would yield no meat. I grew desperate. There was only one alternative. There would still be marauders—men who preyed on others and took their food. I could join one of their bands.

It took me a very long time to find what I was hunting. By nightfall I had seen only a few persons, lone figures moving quickly and warily through the streets. Finally, just as darkness fell, I saw a group of men moving quickly together. They had the look of a hunting party, for they moved steadily, peering from side to side as they went. I kept out of sight until they were well ahead, then followed. They were large men—nearly as tall as I—and they looked strong and aggressive. That they had maintained their strength meant they were good hunters, but that strength posed difficulties for me. I would not be able to drive them from their booty. If there had been only one or two, it might have been possible, but four strong men would not be intimidated. I kept on their trail nonetheless. We needed food and I would have to find a way to get it.

They hunted through the night, going from gate to gate, house to house. But they found only decayed corpses and skeletons, their bones long ago picked clean by the rats. Several times I thought of leaving them, but each time I remembered the cries of the baby and the pinched, drawn look of Xiyou's face. There were dark circles under her eyes, and her arms had become painfully thin.

Suddenly the men stopped and I crouched in a doorway, watching them. The moon had risen and the wind died so that now it only blew in gusts, whisking the dust along the ground in fits and starts. One of the men had detected something and the others were waiting for him to give them a direction to move in. I scanned the horizon but could see nothing except empty walls and gates. If the man saw something, his eyes were keener than mine. He pointed in a direction to the northwest—away from the center of town—and the four broke into a trot. I followed.

They moved quickly through the empty streets, stopping now and then while the leader studied the roadway, then moving on. I wondered whether they heard something I did not. The night was quiet and men with hearing sharpened by months of predation could read the sounds of the night like a book.

The men began running, and I knew the prey must be nearby. Then I noticed the smell: it was smoke, given off by a coal fire. They had detected it miles away and were homing in. Just a night earlier they would not have been able to do this because of the strong and shifting winds, but tonight the winds were calmer and the smoke drew them on like a beacon.

A strange feeling began to go through me and a shiver ran down my spine. The walls I was gliding past were familiar ones. I had often passed this way before.

I rounded a corner recklessly, no longer able to hold myself in check. Not fifty feet ahead the men had stopped in front of a gate. And behind that gate were a small child and two women.

It was easier for them to enter than I had ever imagined. They did not waste time pounding at the gate. One of them removed a lever from his belt and pushed it between the doors of the gate; he shoved it upward and I could hear the cross bar fall to the ground. Then the men were through the gate.

For a moment I was paralyzed. There seemed no way

to prevent what was going to happen. My impulse was to rush into the courtyard, but I held myself back. That would be foolish. The men would overpower me in a matter of moments and then our plight would be hopeless.

I glided to the wall and waited just outside the gate. Muffled screams came from the house. Crouched low, I darted through the courtyard. When I entered the house my senses reeled. The woman was lying in a corner, unconscious, blood streaming from her mouth; the child lay at her side, crying loudly; and Xiyou was pinned to the floor, naked, held by three men while the fourth raped her.

I raised the iron rod I had used to kill rats and split the rapist's skull like a melon; with the second swing I crushed the cheek of another man. Then two of them were on me, pummeling and kicking me. One grasped the lever he had used to open the gate and swung it at me, striking me squarely on the shoulder. I crumpled to my knees, numbed by the pain, but did not drop my rod.

We faced each other. The men began to circle, trying to get behind me. One leaped at me, and at the same time I felt the arms and shoulder of his accomplice plow into me from behind, knocking me helplessly off balance. Then I was on the ground, rolling madly as the man with the lever slashed it down at my head again and again.

One of his blows struck my wrist, and with a cry of pain I dropped my rod. One man pinned me to the ground while the other stood and lifted his weapon high, ready to deal out a finishing blow.

There was a sudden crash and the man sank to the ground, his head bleeding, Xiyou collapsing beside him. Somehow she had found the strength to swing the rod I had dropped. The other man's attention wavered for a second, distracted by the sudden blow out of nowhere, and in that second I was on him, striking him first in the jaw, then in the forehead with the iron rod. With a groan he collapsed.

Two of the men were dead, the others so maimed that they would probably not survive. I carried the bodies of those still alive a hundred yards to a cross street, then fifty yards down it. If they had the strength to live they could crawl away.

The woman was hurt badly—I guessed she had a concussion—but she would recover. Xiyou was terrified and bruised, but the harm was more psychological than physical. My shoulder felt broken. When I tried to move it the pain was excruciating, and it had turned dark blue and begun to swell.

The ashes of the fire that had been used to boil water and had led the marauders to the house were still smoking. I scattered them on the ground, then came back into the house and lay down on the platform and tried to sleep. I dozed off but woke when I rolled over onto my shoulder. From the other side of the platform came the soft, muted sound of weeping. It was the sound that a wounded child makes. Xiyou was crying.

Chapter Twenty-Five

After the attack, Xiyou kept to herself. She would look at no one. She seemed to have taken the blame for the attack on herself. Had she not been the one who lit the fire even though I had warned her against doing so? Was it not her fault, then, that the woman was still delirious and dizzy and could not walk more than a few steps without sitting? And had it not been for her error, would my shoulder not be sound instead of a lump of swollen purple flesh? She was disoriented and sat for hours, staring into space; then she would begin cleaning the house, sweeping and sweeping even when nothing needed to be done. She cleaned our one pot over and over again. All this was done in a frenzy. Then she would sit on the edge of the sleeping platform, in the corner farthest from the rest of us, and stare into space.

Every second day I went out with my sack and rod and returned, toward sundown, with the mangled bodies of a few rats. Now they were smaller, harder to find; but their flesh was keeping us alive.

This went on for weeks. The woman recovered her strength; although my shoulder was still tender I could move it; Xiyou remained a shell.

The weather began to change more quickly now. The wind softened and the dust storms decreased. For a few days there was actually rain. The woman and child took to sitting outside in the courtyard. A few times we had heard cries in the night, but mostly there was only a deathlike silence, punctuated by the twitter of birds circling overhead.

And then a stroke of luck turned my way. It happened on a day when I had given up all hope. I wandered into the center of town again and saw a truck with three soldiers sitting in it.

I approached them cautiously. They were asleep, but when I rapped on the door they wakened.

"You must have come from Urumchi or Hami," I said.

The driver looked at me and nodded with a peculiar expression on his face. The men exchanged words; then one of them asked to see my papers. I told him I had none.

"You are a foreigner," he said, as if it was an accusation.

"I'm Canadian," I replied. "But what does that matter. Look around. The town is filled with corpses of dying people. They need food."

The men exchanged glances again; then one of them got out of the truck and told me to get in.

The driver started the truck and drove slowly through the town and out into the desert. We passed the PLA barracks and then headed east. After twenty minutes I asked where we were going.

"Hami," said the driver, nothing more.

I thought of Xiyou and the woman and child back in Liuyuan. Who would give them food? Who would protect them?

"There are others in Liuyuan who depend on me," I said. "They will die if I don't return."

"You are a foreigner," said the driver. "Do you have a Chinese family?"

The others laughed. Then I knew there was nothing left to do but go where they wanted to take me. My only hope was that there I could find someone to listen to my tale.

It took us two days to reach Hami. There I was given food and allowed to sleep. The next day two soldiers came for me. The first official they took me to offered me a chair and a cup of tea.

"Could you tell me your story," he said. "My comrades have told me some details, but I must hear more. I am told you speak Chinese well."

He smiled as he spoke; it was half a grin, awkward and a little tense.

"I came from Liuyuan," I said.

"That is a long way," said the man, appraising me coolly.

"Yes," I said. "It is a long way. There are people in Liuyuan who are starving. They have had no food for months."

"You have no passport," said the man. Again he gave me his awkward grin.

"I lost it," I said. "I was on a train that was stopped when the flood washed away the track. We tried to cross the desert and there was a great storm. Soldiers found us and took us to Liuyuan. My passport lies somewhere in the desert."

The man made a note on a piece of paper.

"Nationality?" he said. His eyes were on me, studying my face, waiting for something that would confirm a suspicion.

"Canadian," I said.

"Do you remember the number of your passport and where and when it was issued?" he asked.

"A–927541," I said. "It was issued in Windsor, Ontario, in July 1959."

He made another note.

"When did you enter China?"

I told him, also where.

"We will check this," he said. "Meanwhile you must stay in your hotel."

"The people in Liuyuan need food," I said. "They are starving and prey on each other like wild animals."

He made another note, then, with a wave of his hand, dismissed me.

The two soldiers accompanied me back to the hotel. I told them I was hungry, and they took me to a restaurant and stood just inside the door while I ate. One of them spoke to a waiter, who turned to stare at me; then the waiter said something and they both laughed.

I slept uneasily that night. I could not get Xiyou and the woman and child out of my mind. When I left the hotel for breakfast the next morning, the soldiers were gone, but there were two new men, probably security police, who followed me. One of them was a short, stocky man who looked tougher and more efficient than his comrade. I could sense the professional—he was like a cat, ready to spring if I tried to run.

By noon my nerves were shot. I tried to tell myself that the people in Liuyuan had waited for months and that a few more days would not matter, but I kept thinking of Xiyou and the bands of marauders still roaming the streets.

After lunch I went to the government building again. This time the man in the office did not smile when I came in.

"We are checking your passport through the Canadian embassy in Beijing," he said. "You will have to be patient."

I told him that I was not concerned about my passport but that there were people starving in Liuyuan, and I wanted to know what was being done.

A pained expression crossed his face, as if I had spoken about something unclean—incest or pedophilia. There was an awkward silence.

"Each day people die there," I said. "Don't you care?"

He looked up and our eyes met; there was a blank expression in his eyes, almost as if he did not see me.

"They need food and medical supplies," I said. "The army should be sent to restore order. Many have died but many still live."

He said nothing. We sat in silence and then he began writing on a piece of paper on his desk. After five minutes passed he looked up again. The expression was the same, neither surprise nor outrage. He would wait me out, that was all.

I left the office and began to walk down the hallway, then stopped and headed in the other direction, past office after office. Finally I found the one I wanted. There were no signs, nothing but numbers, but it was the last office in the hallway. The man inside could be either very low or very high on the totem pole.

It was hard to tell at first. He wore a blue coat, but they all wore blue coats. He was older than the first man, his face lined, his hair graying, but that could also mean nothing. He had a large stack of papers on his desk, but so did every Chinese bureaucrat.

"I am Canadian," I said.

He nodded.

"I have come from Liuyuan," I said.

"From Gansu," he replied.

"Yes, Gansu," I said. "The people in Liuyuan are starving. The government must send relief—food, soldiers."

He made a notation on a piece of paper; then he picked up the phone on his desk and dialed. I heard him tell my story into the receiver and watched him listen to the reply. Then he hung up and made another notation on the piece of paper before him.

I waited, hoping, but he said nothing. Several minutes passed.

"Will you send relief?" I asked finally. I had the feeling that I was a character in some absurd dream where people talked and gestured but never made contact.

I stood and looked down at him. He wrote on, making character after character on sheets of lined paper.

"You must send a relief column!" I said. "People are starving! Comrades dying! Good Communists!"

"Liuyuan is in Gansu," he said. "We are responsible only for towns in Xinjiang."

In the afternoon I walked through the streets. The men followed me. Finally I bought a bottle of brandy, went back to my room, and got drunk and slept until ten. When I woke I was famished and went out again.

I had walked for an hour before I finally accepted the fact that it was too late to find a place to eat. Most of the buildings were darkened. The few where lights glittered were houses. Hami was not very rich in nightlife, but then neither was Urumchi or Shanghai or Beijing. People were not to be corrupted—whether they wished to be or not. Their everyday life was as exciting as rice gruel. How could they stand it? And why did they stand it?

I returned to my room and lay down again. Somehow it felt better to be inside, alone, rather than walking the streets trailed by two men. Here at least I could be alone with my thoughts.

I would keep trying, but if nothing worked, then I would leave the city and return to Beijing. They were watching me, but it would be child's play to lose them. I could get a train east, change my appearance between Hami and the next station so that I looked like a Chinese, buy another ticket, and travel on unobserved. Then when I reached Beijing I would speak to the officials about Liuyuan. And if they wouldn't listen, there were always the foreign journalists. They would gobble the story up and then something would happen. To save Chinese lives I would probably have to use western newspapers. It was a colossal absurdity.

The next morning after breakfast I went back to the government building, back to the office of the first man I had spoken to. This time irritation showed in his eyes through the professional indifference. He listened to me, made more notes, then told me that my passport was still being investigated.

"The Canadian embassy has not responded yet," he said, looking at me with smug satisfaction.

An alarm tripped off in the back of my mind. The delay might mean nothing, but it could also mean that the Canadian embassy was consulting the Agency before acting. And that could mean almost anything, the worst being a denial that I was a Canadian citizen.

I could imagine the reaction in the Agency office when the message came through from the Canadians. First there would be a momentary panic, then a meeting. The director of Far East operations, an aging Ivy Leaguer called Hildebrand who still wore shirts with button-down collars, would sit at a table and discuss the possible meanings of the request that the Chinese government had made. It could mean that I was captured, my cover blown, and they were probing, trying to get a response from the American side. Hildebrand was a specialist in cold, impersonal logic. His conclusion would be very simple. The Chinese had me, and if the American government admitted I was a citizen, then the Chinese would announce to the world that they had captured another spy. The course of action that the agency should take would be obvious: deny any knowledge of me. If I were not an American, then I could not be an American spy. The others would nod agreement, men I had known for years, had had lunch with, played tennis and golf with. McCracken, whose oldest kid was the best pitcher in the Alexandria midget league because I had taught him to throw a curveball; Cavenna, whom I had sat up half the night with, listening to him moan about an unfaithful wife; Sturdivant, who spent weekends with his latest conquest from the secretarial pool at the cottage I owned on the Maryland shore—none of them would say a thing when Hildebrand came to his conclusion. We were all expendable, every one of us—it was the law of the Agency, the inexorable logic of the profession we had chosen. "Tough break," they would say later, when they talked about it over drinks. "Hildebrand's a heartless bastard; he'd sell his own mother down the river if he thought it was for the good of the Agency." But no one would lift a finger to oppose him.

Suddenly I was aware that the man was speaking again and that I had missed part of what he was saying.

". . . have investigated. Found nothing."

"What?" I said.

"The officials in Gansu have investigated your statements. They say that there is no problem in Liuyuan, that the people have enough food."

I fixed him with a stare.

"Your worries are groundless," he said. "The Chinese People's Republic would never allow its citizens to starve. Such things have never happened since Liberation."

I rose and started to leave.

"You must stay in your room after sunset," he said. "The air in the city is unhealthy at night."

I nodded and went out into the hall. The two comrades who were following me frowned. They had been leaning against the wall, half asleep, and now they would have to walk again.

By the time I reached the hotel I had it all worked out. First I would need a train schedule, then some clothes and makeup. The rest would not be hard, but I would have to move fast. At the moment I was still only a troublesome Canadian without a passport. If the embassy formally denied knowledge of me, I would be in another category, and then it would be a hundred times more difficult to do what I had to do.

Chapter Twenty-Six

Night fell. I waited until eight, then went to the door and opened it. The guards were opposite, squatting, their backs braced against the wall. One was sleeping, the other watching the door. I nodded to him, then walked out into the hallway, down to the central desk, and out onto the street.

I began to wander, moving down the main avenue, stopping at each street as if I were looking for a restaurant. I did not look behind me. They were there—there was no need to verify their presence.

I entered a crowded restaurant and ordered mutton. The waiter brought it: a greasy leg of mutton on a bed of rice. I tried to eat, but the taste was too rank—the mutton had probably sat half a day in a truck, then two more days in an unrefrigerated storeroom.

My tails were standing at the door. It was warm and they were drowsy. I left the restaurant and quickened my pace, heading up a side street lined with the walls of courtyards, gleaming white in the moonlight.

An alley snaked off to the right, twisting into the darkness of faceless buildings. I turned down it and broke into a run. They came on behind me, huffing and puffing.

The professional was the stronger runner of the two—his strides were clipped and regular. The other ran wildly, and I could hear him gasping for air.

A dozen houses circled a square. I slid into the doorway of the first and waited. They appeared, running out of the street into the square, with tongues lolling like two spent hounds, and passed within five feet of me.

I waited for thirty seconds, each second a lifetime, then turned and ran back up the street in the direction I had come from. Twice I stumbled in the darkness but my pace did not flag. I was heading toward the center of the city and the train station.

I wanted to find a hiding place near the station and hole up until morning; then I could disguise myself and board a train as a Chinese. It was a simple plan, but its beauty lay in its simplicity. One Chinese among eight hundred million: to find me would be like looking for a needle in a haystack.

Dawn found me shivering with cold. I was crouched beside the wall of a deserted building. The air was balmy—a strange sort of dampness caused by the chilly night air and the first heat of day. I felt weak, and when I stood I found that I was unsteady. I needed food or I would not get far, but first I had to find something to darken the color of my skin and hair.

Near the station there was a small department store. I bought a large envelope, a pen, and a satchel, then went to the counter that sold cosmetics and asked for hair dye and skin cream. The woman peered at me strangely and asked me to repeat myself. I thought she was having difficulty because of my Chinese and did as she asked, but at the same time I became worried. There might be something behind her question besides mere curiosity.

When I left the department store I went to a grocery store and bought some apples and several pieces of flat bread and some ground cinnamon. I planned to eat the apples and the bread on the train—the cinnamon could be mixed with the skin cream. The result would be crude, but if I reapplied the cream often enough it would be adequate.

The city was alive with people now, the streets crowded. Twice I had seen policemen; each time my heart started to race, but they did not seem to notice me. But I had no place to use the hair dye and skin cream, and time was passing. The longer I waited the more people who would be looking for me.

In an empty street I crouched down by the wall of a courtyard and mixed the cinnamon with the cream and rubbed it into the skin of my face and hands. There was a pump at the head of the street. I broke off a chunk of the dye and added some water to it, using my hands as a cup. Then I rubbed it into my hair. As a final step I rubbed dust on my clothes and the satchel.

In a post office near the station I mailed the envelope. Inside were the documents I had picked up in Turpan. I addressed it to Mr. Franklin Pierce, c/o the Friendship Hotel, Beijing. That hotel kept mail addressed to foreigners for months; it sat on a board where anyone could claim it. The system was sloppy and usually the hotel clerk did not even require identification. Unless the real Franklin Pierce showed up at the Friendship Hotel the documents would be waiting for me when I arrived. I used a pencil to make two faint lines across the flap. If the letter had been opened I would be able to tell. It was a reckless move, but the odds were a lot better than those I would have if the Chinese found the documents in my possession.

The clock above the ticket counter in the crowded station said nine forty-five. Beneath it was a blackboard where the times of arrivals and departures were indicated. A train for Xi'an left at ten ten; another for Urumchi at noon. I had to get on that first train.

The long queue moved slowly. My eyes kept moving to the clock, then the doorway of the station. At any moment policemen would appear. They would expect me to try to board the train for Xi'an and would come in two groups: plainclothes men and uniformed. The first group were probably already inside the station, waiting for someone to do something that looked suspicious.

There were still a dozen men in front of me and it was almost ten. I could not risk a disturbance by pushing to the head of the line. Anything that drew attention to me could be fatal. I left the line and went out to the platform, hoping that in the crush of passengers I could board the train, then buy a ticket from a conductor.

The train pulled into the station and the crowd moved toward the cars. I stayed in the middle, pushing doggedly ahead, crushed between two families. They were weighted down with boxes and children, and moved slowly but steadily toward the car like a juggernaut.

The conductor stood at the bottom of the steps, inspecting tickets. She was a tall, stern-looking woman, and she demanded each person show a ticket before she would let him pass. I had to find a way to move her or I would never get aboard.

Already the crowd behind me had thinned and most of the passengers had boarded. Three men stood just outside the door of the ticket office, studying the crowd. They were well-dressed and strong-looking: doubtless secret police. If I was left on the platform when the train pulled away I would stand out like a sore thumb.

One of the old women did not have a ticket, and an argument between the family and the conductor broke out. A bell clanged and the conductors guarding the entrances of the other cars stepped inside and closed the doors.

The argument grew louder, and the engine tooted its whistle. Still the conductor would not yield. Suddenly the train began to move slowly, and the family made a final rush toward the doorway, pushing the conductor before them. I stayed in their midst.

I was on the train. The argument continued in the vestibule above the doorway as the train slowly picked up speed. I saw my chance and slid past the conductor and onto the car.

In the crowded hard-berth car, I squeezed into a place between two old women. We had left the city behind and had entered the desert. It flew past, a blur of brown-yellow beneath a bright blue sky. I shut my eyes and tried to sleep. There would be problems ahead, but at least I had cleared the first hurdle.

I woke early in the afternoon. The car was unbearably hot. The doors at both ends were open, but the train was moving slowly and the breeze was almost nil.

We were climbing through yellow hills that gradually gave way to mountains. The engine seemed to be straining. Outside the sun beat down unmercifully. The hills were dotted with caves. Some had doorways; others were merely holes carved in earth. People sat in the shadow of the entrances. Sometimes we passed so close to them that I could see their faces and the expressions of curiosity on them as they watched the train pass.

The train seemed to reach the summit, passed through

a narrow valley, then began to descend. The track made a great curve of almost a hundred and eighty degrees, the last few cars of our train visible, riding on the elevated roadbed on the other side of a small lake. Then we plunged into a dark tunnel. In two hours we would reach Lanchou. I would speak to the conductor then and buy a ticket for Xi'an. She would be angry, but by the end of the day she would be too tired to be suspicious.

The train emerged from the tunnel into bright sunlight. I shut my eyes and tried to sleep again. It was going to be easy. There would be a mess at the end, in Beijing, but that could be managed. I would not even bother with the officials. The foreign journalists stayed at the Minzu Hotel; I could have dinner there and tell them my story. The Agency contact at the Canadian Embassy would arrange for a new passport. Even if the word had been given to disavow me, he would produce the documents I needed if I was not in custody. A clean escape would be preferable to allowing the Chinese to capture me. Before the story about Liuyuan broke, I would be in the States. I would probably read about it in the airport in San Francisco.

We steamed into Xi'an at eight. The sky was still pink to the west, but ahead of us the stars were already twinkling in the eastern sky. The train slowed as we entered the station, and I took my suitcase and walked toward the end of the car. The conductor had told me that there would be a connecting train for Beijing at midnight. She had been so tired that she did not even bother to look at me when I had approached her for the ticket.

The train stopped and I climbed down the steps and started across the platform. Suddenly two men were beside me. I could have struggled but it would have only made things worse.

The jail they took me to was located somewhere in the middle of town. It was an ancient town and the building smelled of dry rot. The cell was dark and damp. During the night rats ran across the floor. In the corner there was a hole where I could relieve myself. The smell that rose from it filled the cell.

I had no documents, nothing to show why I had come or what I was doing. The first thing I did when they put me in the cell was to rub the cream off my face and hands. There was a jug of water in the corner, and I doused myself with this and rubbed my hair. Some of the dye came off. In the morning, when they questioned me, I would look like a westerner. My story would be simple: I had been scared and had run. Others had done as much before. If the embassy had acknowledged me, the authorities would first criticize, then extradite me. If the embassy had not, I would be questioned further. That could mean a lot of things, but it would do no good to worry about them.

Chapter Twenty-Seven

An hour after the sun rose the cell door clinked open and a guard appeared with a bowl of rice gruel and tea. The morning air was cool and I was shivering, but the food and tea warmed me. When I finished eating I paced back and forth in the tiny cell for ten minutes to get my circulation going, then lay back down on the cot and stretched out with my hands behind my head and watched the small patch of blue sky I could see through the window.

About ten the door opened again and the guard reappeared, took the bowls away, and left. Immediately two men entered the room. One was young, neatly groomed, fat and sleek. The other was older, his skin lined, his hair thinning. Three chairs were brought in and the sleek man nodded toward one and I sat.

"You have traveled far," he said. "From—" he looked at a piece of paper he had brought with him "—from Liuyuan."

I nodded.

"Traveling without a passport is difficult to do in China," he said, "but you seem to do it quite well."

I gave him a half smile.

"Perhaps you have had practice at this sort of thing before?" he said.

"I've never lost my passport before," I replied.

Now it was his turn to smile.

"What would you have done if you had reached Beijing?" asked the man. "I assume that was your destination."

"Go to the embassy, of course. I could not wait forever in Hami."

He nodded and exchanged glances with his partner.

"Tell us something about yourself. Where do you come from in Canada and what kind of work do you do there?"

The details of the lost passport flashed through my mind. The embassy would have them; if they did verify me they would do so using those facts.

"I'm a businessman from Windsor," I said.

"Liuyuan is a strange place to do business," he replied. "Few foreigners ever travel there."

"It was not of my choosing," I said. "The flood disrupted the railway."

"There are many different kinds of businessmen," said the older man. "Tell us what kind of business you do."

His English was not as good as the first man's, and his voice was hoarse. Now, as he spoke, he peered at me with eyes that seemed to bore into me.

"I'm with a company that makes heavy machinery," I said.

The man took some cigarettes from the pocket of his shirt and offered me one. I took it and he lit it for me, then took one for himself. He didn't offer the younger man one.

"If you stayed in Hami, none of this would have happened," he said. "Tell us, please, why you did not."

I stared back at him. Something in his glance was unsettling, almost challenging—I was damned if he would make me look away.

"I was tired of waiting," I said. "I've been waiting for months—since the flood—and I was tired. A man gets tired sometimes. You understand that, don't you?"

The man nodded and took a long drag on his cigarette.

"The men in Hami are bureaucrats," I continued. "They do things in a slow, bureaucratic way. Westerners have no patience for that. No man would if he had wandered back and forth over the desert for a month. There is a limit to any man's patience."

"The flood brought bad times to Gansu and Xinjiang—we understand that. The conditions were bad, and for that we apologize. China is a poor country."

"I did not care about the conditions," I said. "But the men in Hami would not listen. Did they tell you about Liuyuan?"

He shook his head.

"Before the great flood it was a town of several thousand. Now the population is much smaller. The people have no food there—they eat the flesh of rats."

"You have seen this with your own eyes?" he said.

"I lived in Liuyuan for four months," I said.

He looked toward the younger man, who nodded and wrote something down.

"Almost five months have passed since the flood," I said. "The army has deserted the town—the leaders have gone with them. The people live on without medicine and food. How can responsible officials allow this to happen?"

"The situation in Liuyuan may be bad," he said. "Of this I do not know. But that is not our concern. We will look into it, but first we must know more about you. Your embassy has not answered our questions yet. You may have lost your passport—the story is logical—but until we have information from your embassy we must detain you. You can understand this."

He was looking at me again with the same hard, penetrating stare.

"Surely you have a better place to keep me than this," I said. "I have committed no crime. I don't want to be treated as a criminal."

"There is no hotel in the town," said the sleek one. "We have no alternative."

He said the words easily, without any expression, as if they were completely true, but we both knew he was lying.

"I must tell you that the situation is serious," the sleek one continued. "To travel without a passport in China is a grave offense. If your embassy does not acknowledge our message soon, then we will have no choice but to place you on trial. That could be most unpleasant."

"You would try me for traveling without a passport?" I said, feigning a chuckle.

"We would try you as a spy," he said.

"As a spy!" I laughed.

"I can assure you that is no laughing matter," said the sleek one. "The punishment for spies is severe under the people's laws."

"Surely you cannot believe such nonsense," I said, looking at the older man. "If I were a spy would I have gone to the authorities in Hami?"

The man blew smoke through his nostrils but said nothing.

"The Chinese court is lenient with those who confess their crimes," said the sleek one. "Those who admit their errors before trial receive lighter sentences. We try to re-educate them. But once the trial has begun, this privilege is withdrawn."

I laughed again. It was a bit hollow, but I don't think they noticed this. They were suspicious, but they needed more than suspicion. If they were too rough with me they might find themselves in difficulty later. An angry official, embarrassed by the actions of his subordinates, could ruin a man's career. People had been sent to Qinghai Province for less. The safest policy for them was to go slowly until they were sure of themselves; then, if they had the information they needed, they could be as rough as they wanted. That would also please their superiors. A man whose subordinates treated a spy with the severity that his offenses deserved could be certain that his superiors would applaud. It showed that he had instilled the right spirit in his unit. Such a man was a credit to the people—he would be considered the next time a position in the ministry fell vacant.

The older man offered me a cigarette; then he nodded to the younger man, who stood up and left.

We smoked in silence for a few minutes. The cigarettes tasted like burning leaves and I coughed.

"Our tobacco has more flavor than yours," he said, "but for some it's too strong."

"I have not smoked in months," I said. "I had my last cigarette on the train before it stopped in the desert. In Liuyuan there were no cigarettes."

"Tell me what happened there," the man said.

I stood and walked to the side of the cell by the doorway; then leaned my back against it and faced him.

"I was brought to the city by soldiers. They rescued me in the desert. There were hundreds of people, all trying to cross the desert—our train could go no farther, and our food and water were growing less day by day. Many perished but some were saved—the strongest. In Liuyuan things were better . . . at first. But then the food war gone there too, and the people changed. The police could do nothing. The soldiers left. People roamed the streets like wolves."

The man's cigarette was now only a stub; he dropped it on the floor, crushed it out, and lit another.

"I heard stories of such things in my youth," he said. "I lived in Sichuan before Liberation and there were years when the harvest was poor and the landlords took all. People ate their mules and then their watchdogs."

His voice was calm and his face a stiff mask, but his eyes gave him away.

"There is still time to save those who remain in Liuyuan," I said.

He rose and moved to the door.

"I will do what I can," he said, and left.

The door clanked shut behind him and the key was turned in the lock. I lay back down on the bed and stared at the sky again. The man had left a pack of cigarettes and some matches on the window ledge and I lit one. I was calmer than I had been in a long time. Something would be done. This man was not like the others. I did not know how I knew this, but I was certain.

Chapter Twenty-Eight

THEY came again the next morning. This time the questions were all about Hami: how I had gotten there, how I had left. We continued to fence. I had simply left, I said. I mentioned nothing about the men following me. We played the game: they did not admit that I had been followed; I, that I had eluded the tail. It was all nice and polite and meant nothing and all three of us knew it. We were stalling for time: they were waiting for word from the Canadian embassy; I was resting, building my strength up for what I knew would come. It had been five days since inquiry had been made at the Canadian embassy. My passport number was red-flagged there; an embassy officer would have been in contact with Washington fifteen minutes after he received the inquiry from the Chinese. Washington would have stalled for a day, maybe two, while they made up their minds, but no longer. If there had been no reply by this time it meant only one thing: Hildebrand had decided to write me off. Silence was the Agency's answer. My file would be placed in the drawer marked "inoperative," and someone would be given the job of contacting my relatives to tell them to be certain to report any mysterious attempts made to contact them. When agents were broken, the other side usually tried to use their families.

I walked back and forth in the cell three times a day for half an hour each time. In between I lay on the cot and stared at the sky or smoked the cigarettes the older interrogator left behind. I wondered what his name was. Probably Wang or Wei or Gao—a common name, for he looked like a common man: simple, direct. The younger, sleek one was a different sort. He was probably a Communist because it was expedient. The same type existed in the west. You could see them at every political convention or board meeting. They did what they ought to do because that was what they thought would get them ahead. Instead of honest emotion they had a bend in their minds, a shunt of sorts, that allowed them to channel off their feelings to the perimeter of their souls so that their sleep and peace of mind and self-respect were not disturbed. Hildebrand belonged to the same club.

"Our government is concerned with spies. You must know this."

The older interrogator was speaking. His expression was stern.

"Spies?" I said, exaggerating the note of incredulity. "What would Canadians want to spy on in China? your soldiers with tennis shoes and old rifles—your airplanes that can't cross the ocean—your bombs that are more dangerous to you than us?"

He lit a cigarette and blinked as the smoke rose to his eyes.

"You play games," he said. "You think that I do not know this, but I do. You are skillful but do not press your luck too far."

Our eyes met. He held the pack of cigarettes toward me, but I shook my head.

"You haven't asked me yet if I am Russian," I said. "You have been slow. I thought you would ask that the first day."

He made a sound that was halfway between a chuckle and a laugh.

"You try to provoke me but you will not succeed. Tell me again why you left Hami—that is what I must know. You said you had no patience for the ways of bureaucrats—is that right?"

"For bureaucrats who would not listen when I told them of Liuyuan," I said. "One acted as if the place did not exist. Another claimed that he was responsible only for towns in Xinjiang."

He shook his head. "We have many of that kind. They wear blinders before their eyes and hide behind the stack of papers on their desks and the political slogans they mouth at party meetings. Such men harm China—they have always harmed China. It is from them and their kind that Mao tried to liberate us, but they are still with us. Like ticks they grow fat on our blood."

"What has been done in Liuyuan?" I asked.

"I have contacted the party leader in Jiayuquan. He is a good man—a responsible man. He will make certain that something is done."

"How could such a thing happen?" I said.

He shook his head, stood, and stared at the patch of sky beyond the window. I wondered how men like him accepted it all—the crazy contradictions and inconsistencies, the gross hypocrisy, the fact that in the People's Republic, people did not count for much.

The next day he came again. Now his questions were more direct. Who had I traveled across the desert with? How long had it taken? Why had I fled from Hami? The last question came up again and again, and each time I stuck to my original story: that I had simply become impatient and left.

At noon, when my bowl of rice and tea were brought, he stayed.

"The food is not very good," he said.

"An understatement," I answered between mouthfuls.

"And yet it is not so bad as that I once had in the prison of the Kuomintang."

"When?" I asked without looking up.

"In 1947, during the war for liberation, I was in a squadron that was captured. We were given one cup of tea and a bowl of rice every three days. Strong men were reduced to skeletons. Many died."

"But you survived," I said, matter-of-factly.

"Yes, I survived. The Kuomintang were forced to move on and they left us behind after turning their machine guns on us. I lay for three days before the peasants found me. It was a miracle that I lived."

"Many suffered during those times," I said.

"Many," he repeated. "Soldiers and peasants alike. The Kuomintang robbed and raped wherever they passed. They took the food of the peasants and raped their wives and daughters and in the end it was this that brought about their downfall. The people would not follow those who preyed upon them."

"Poetic justice," I said.

"What?"

"The gods punished them for their misdeeds with defeat," I said.

"God had little to do with it," he said. "Officially God was on the side of the Kuomintang, for the religious leaders of the country prayed for them. Christians always believed in Chiang Kai-shek. They did not trust us."

"Many mistakes were made," I said.

"Yes," he replied, "many mistakes. Tell me again about Liuyuan—about those you left behind."

I told him of Xiyou and the woman and child.

"They will be rescued," he said. "Today I talked again with the leader in Jiayuguan. He told me that trucks with soldiers and food were sent two days ago. By now they will have reached Liuyuan."

"Where will those they rescue be taken?" I asked.

"Jiayuguan," he said. "You are concerned for the girl?"

"She has been wounded in the mind," I said. "She can not care for herself."

"Her family will be notified and one of them will come for her," he said. "You can do nothing more than you have done."

I knew he was right, but for some reason I did not want to give up my stewardship. Always it had seemed that in the end we would be back together again, even if for only a short while. Now I realized that I would never see her again, and the idea upset me.

"This woman was more than a friend to you," he said. "I can see that. In China such things are difficult. Better for you and for her that you let her find her own way. You have enough problems before you without adding that one. Already those who check such matters are disturbed with the delay in the embassy's response to our request. Justice moves swiftly in China. Within another week they will demand that you be placed on trial."

"What will their evidence be?" I asked.

"They will not need evidence," he said. "It is you who will need evidence to prove your innocence."

Chapter Twenty-Nine

On the next day he was graver still.

"The authorities press me," he said. "I cannot stop them any longer. The trial is set for one week from today."

A chill ran through me. At least they did not have the papers I had mailed: that would have sealed my doom.

"If you confess now, it will be much easier," he said. "Then I can seek leniency for you."

"Confess what?" I said. "That I committed the crime of traveling without a passport?"

He frowned, then made a motion with his hands that indicated he was through with the matter.

"You do not understand the gravity of the situation—and you do not know what we know," he said. Now I could feel his eyes on me, watching, waiting for something that would give me away.

Abruptly he stood and left and I was alone. I lay down on the cot and stared out the window. He had done his job well: the seed was planted. I could not know what they knew. Perhaps they had intercepted the mail—possibly the people in the post office had seized the envelope and identified me as the sender. But I had been disguised—or had I? I could not remember. It was a simple thing: I had a clear mind—I did not forget things like that. Why couldn't I remember now?

I stood up and began pacing back and forth in the tiny cell. I was panicking, acting like a fool—a rank amateur. It was the oldest tactic in the world: scare your victim, offer him the hope of escape from a certain and horrible fate, and he will snap at it like a hungry fish. Then he will be hooked, and you can reel him in and slit him open. I was too experienced for that to work on me. Who did they think they were dealing with, anyway?

I tried to calm myself. I was losing my grip and playing into their hands. Perhaps it had been the long months in Liuyuan, the journeys across the desert. Something had happened to me. I had been through ten times worse than this in Poland, and once, in East Germany—that was something I did not want to think about, because every time I did I became sick to my stomach. In all those times I had never cracked; now, without any real pressure, my feelings were in chaos.

I began to wonder about the interrogator. He was sympathetic but also a party man. If it were a question of human values versus party obligations, the human values would mean nothing.

I lay down again and wondered for the thousandth time why I was here. What strange, self-destructive quirk had driven me down this road? What had made me join the Agency in the first place? A sense of adventure? The salary? The work made a man strange. He had no steady friends and he could not build a normal life. He roamed the world like a vagabond, and in the end he was thrown away like a worn-out shoe.

In the afternoon I tried to sleep but I couldn't. I had to do something to calm myself, so I started to think about people I knew, about their faces and their gestures, hoping to find one that seemed sympathetic. I knew a dozen women with varying degrees of intimacy, but they were just faces and breasts and thighs—laughter—but nothing more. I had the same lukewarm feeling about men I had grown up with, worked with, lived with through crises. None of them would risk much for me, nor I for them. I felt a certain warmth for one or two, but nothing more. Then I thought of Xiyou.

The last time I had seen her she had been only an empty shell, hardly noticing me, unable to speak or feel anything but confused depression. I could see her eyes now, filled with the haunted emptiness of those whose beliefs have been destroyed, leaving in their stead only a vacuum filled with confusion and despair. She could not help me—she had not strength or cunning enough even to save herself.

I began to feel drowsy. My eyelids drooped and my limbs felt heavy. Sleep was coming on, and with it the oblivion I craved.

The next day the questioners did not come. It turned stiflingly hot, and I sweated and removed my shirt and trousers and lay on the cot trying to keep cool. I had eaten no salt for several days and sweating gave me cramps, then chills.

The day after was the same. The day after that I gave up exercising and lay all day, getting up only to eat or relieve myself.

I began to wonder about the trial. Would there be a jury? A defense lawyer? But that was silly nonsense and I knew it. The whole thing would be a put-up job; I'd be like a virgin in a whorehouse. I imagined myself standing in the dock and proclaiming my innocence. "I am on trial because I tried to help save Chinese people," I would say. "You have forgotten whole villages—thousands starve or become less than human to stay alive. Look to yourselves when you search for guilt."

I went on and on, talking to myself, rehearsing again and again the words I would use. Each time my logic was irrefutable. Their sins were manifest and still they did not listen. Then, finally, I became quieter inside. The imaginary argument reached a crescendo, then died. In its place came the awful realization that I was indeed guilty.

As if in a vision, I saw the envelope I had mailed in Hami held up by the prosecutor. He described the contents. Men looked at me, their eyes filled with hatred.

"He would sell our secrets to our enemies," the prosecutor said. "He pretends to be a friend of the Chinese people but really he is a traitor to their cause. He says he returned to Hami to save the people of Liuyuan, but really he came so that he might complete his act of espionage."

I imagined myself in the dock listening to his words, and with each word I felt more and more alone. I was three thousand miles from my country, forsaken by the people who had sent me, and I was going to be convicted and sentenced. "The punishment for spies is severe under the people's laws." The words came back to me together with the piercing eyes of the interrogator. They will shoot you, I said to myself. You will die in this godforsaken country because of two pieces of paper with a few numbers on them and your stupid need to play God.

The room was empty when they brought me in. There were benches so I assumed that if this was a courtroom and they used it for trials, they sometimes allowed spectators. But my trial was to be different.

I was led to the dock and told to stand—I had no choice, for there was no chair—and then the two white-coated guards walked to the middle of the room, a place halfway between the dock and the stage upon which a long table with chairs sat. Here they stopped, turned, and stood at attention.

Another door opened and five men and a woman filed in. Three men went to the platform and sat at the table. The others went to smaller tables that sat on a lower level. There were two of these. A man and a woman sat at the one on my left, a lone man at the table on the right. This last man was about forty. He had a shamefaced, worried look about him: the kind of look that a person wears if life is too much for him and he has resigned himself to the ordeal and still goes through the motions without believing there is any real purpose in doing so. He was my lawyer.

The three men at the big table were all over sixty. The one on the far left looked very tired and his head kept sagging, as if his neck no longer had the strength to keep it upright. The man in the middle had a square, strong-looking jaw like a bulldog; the one on the right was handsome, his immaculate gray Mao jacket perfectly tailored. They were the judges.

The woman and the man who sat at the table on the left were the prosecuting attorney and her assistant. It amused me that the prosecutor had an assistant and the defense lawyer none, but then many things about the trial were amusing. The prosecutor's hair was done in a box cut, with the ends square. She had bangs and wore glasses when she read her notes. She had lots of notes; in fact, it seemed she had enough for a whole book. I suppose her assistant, an earnest-looking young man, must have prepared them for her. My attorney had a single page of notes.

The trial began and the judge with the bulldog jaw read the indictment. I could understand only part of it, for he read very quickly in a monotone. Then the prosecuting attorney presented her evidence. It was contained on the numberless sheets of paper she removed from her briefcase. I could catch only about half of what she said. The words "spy" and "enemy of the people" were repeated often. I listened hard to learn the evidence against me, but missed it.

I kept waiting for my attorney to say something; after a while I began to suspect he was mute.

The woman read from her notes without interruption for almost forty-five minutes. The tired-looking judge slept for almost twenty minutes. The square-jawed man in the middle stared off into space, and the handsome judge's eyes roamed to my face now and then with a sort of disinterested curiosity. Two or three times I thought I detected a trace of a smile on his face.

Then the woman began asking me questions. Was I a Canadian? I said I was. Why did I have no passport? I said I had lost mine. Why did I leave Hami?

I answered as I had answered the interrogators. Then she asked what information I had stolen to give to the enemies of the Chinese people.

I told her that I was not a spy and that I planned to convey no information to anyone. She asked if my employers had promised me a large sum of money for my "criminal deeds." I said I had an employer who sold heavy machinery, but he paid me only for business matters. She asked if my family was being held captive by the "imperialist, hegemonist, and criminal government" that had induced me to commit the crime of espionage against the glorious People's Republic of China. I said I had no immediate family, but that as far as I knew, my two brothers were reasonably happy.

The judge with the bulldog jaw interrupted her once and asked me to repeat an answer, and when I had finished, the handsome judge took his turn.

He told me of the struggles of the Chinese people to free themselves from foreign domination, and then outlined how the foreign powers sent agents among the people to spread false information and "dampen their revolutionary fervor."

I listened to this as best I could. I was very tired, for I had stood for a long time, and after a while his words seemed to run together into a droning hum.

Finally my attorney spoke. He read from the single sheet of paper he had brought with him, and by this time I was so drowsy that he had been speaking for several minutes before I realized that I was hearing a new voice— one that didn't list my crimes and call for punishment.

The court should consider that I was a poor, misdirected foreigner, he said. I had been raised in a corrupt system and while I was an agent of that system I was also a victim; therefore, while my crimes were indeed serious I was not wholly responsible for them. The court should take this into consideration when they sentenced me, he said.

Then the prosecutor spoke again. This time her voice was filled with indignation. She was angry and expostulated on the folly of treating enemies of the people leniently. This set a bad example, she said. The foreign powers were notorious for the weak-kneed character of their courts. It was common knowledge that none took them seriously. Chinese justice was sterner. It had to be to effectively protect the interests of the people. She hoped the judges would remember this and not let off the treacherous agent of the imperialists and hegemonists—here she pointed at me—with a mere slap on the wrist.

When she had finished, the judges rose and left, and the guards came for me and led me out of the courtroom.

I was taken from the court to a small room that connected with it. There was one chair here and I sat. Up high—too high for a man to peer through—was a window. The walls of the room were gray; they had been recently painted. Evidently the authorities had wanted to spruce up the place for their foreign guest.

The guards stood at the door. They were young men, both about twenty, broad-shouldered and handsome. Their uniforms were pressed and fit well.

I waited in the room for half an hour; then I heard a call and the guards led me back into the courtroom. I stood in the dock and listened while the judge with the bulldog jaw read off an account of my crimes. I was, he said, guilty of trying to fabricate stories about a town in Gansu, tales that weakened the authority of the people's government; this was an attempt to cause unrest and disorder. When he had finished I started to laugh. My attorney tried to silence me, but I couldn't stop.

The sentence was twenty years hard labor, and I was remanded to the custody of court officers who transported me back to my cell for the night. The next morning a half-dozen policemen put me in a truck and drove southwest over the desert in the direction of Qinghai.

Chapter Thirty

For a few days I did not see anything but the back of the truck and the men who were guarding me. They were rotated, four always inside with me, two in the cab in front. The road twisted and turned, and we were thrown from side to side, sometimes clear across the cabin. I could have made a break for freedom then—the guards were tough but not experienced—but if I had escaped from the truck it would have gotten me nothing. Without money or identification in west-central China, a man, particularly an occidental, would be as helpless as a man on a polar icecap. So I relaxed and waited to see what the future would bring.

On the third day we began to climb and the air became noticeably thinner. I felt drowsy and slept. The guards tried to stay awake, but soon it was apparent that they would not be able to. I imagined that the men in the cab ahead were having the same difficulty, and I began to have visions of the truck rolling off a mountain road.

On the fourth day the road leveled out. It was still bumpy, but we were no longer climbing. Toward midnight we started to roll over a section of road that was rougher than any we had encountered so far. The wheels thumped and rumbled and we banged into rock after rock; sometimes the truck stopped altogether. We moved slowly, not more than ten or fifteen miles an hour, but still the springs and wheels took a terrible beating.

Abruptly, we stopped. Someone in the cab shouted and there was an answer from somewhere outside the truck—then we began to roll again. The road was still almost impassable, but now it didn't matter. We had reached our destination.

The back of the truck was opened from the outside and the guards jumped out. Cold air floated in—a peculiar, piercing kind of cold I had never felt before.

Several minutes passed while I sat shivering in the truck; then a soldier appeared and ordered me out. He was not one of the six men who had ridden with me from Xi'an. His skin was darker and his eyes were mere slits above prominent cheekbones. He gestured with his rifle and I moved off, walking across a flat field filled with stones. There was a biting wind blowing, the sky was as black as death, and the stars brighter than I had ever seen them.

The soldier guided me with the point of his rifle to a low building built of rough stones and topped with a roof of corrugated metal that glinted in the moonlight. He rapped on the door and someone within barked an answer. The soldier opened the door and we stepped in.

There was one room in the building. The floor was flagstone, the walls unplastered. A squat iron stove sat in the center, the fire inside glowing orange even though it was summer. On one side of the room were a table and two chairs; on the opposite side, directly beneath the only window, a man was lying in a cot, supporting himself on an elbow and inspecting me. He had the same broad face and prominent cheekbones as the soldier, but he was older and there was a look of intelligence in his eyes. He exchanged words with the soldier in a language I did not understand, then turned his attention to me.

"You will be placed in barracks number two. There you will find a bed and blankets. In the morning I will speak with you. You should rest tonight. You have had a long journey."

The tone was rough, the Chinese not good but serviceable. The sentiments surprised me.

I turned and started for the door.

"You are the first Westerner we have had here," the man said. "We should have much to speak of."

I faced him again and nodded; then the guard led me out into the night, across the field for a distance of about a quarter of a mile, and into a building much like the one I had just left. There were three other men here. They were asleep, and when the light of the lantern the guard was carrying fell on them, one raised his head for a moment, then put it down again.

The guard pointed to a bed on the far side of the room, separated from the others, and waited while I went to it. Then he left, locking the door behind him.

I lay down in the darkness. The room was small but the wind whistling through the cracks in the stone walls kept the air fresh. For a man who had had no exercise for almost five days I was amazingly tired. In a few moments I was fast asleep.

The door of the cabin was still closed and the lone window covered with a cloth, but the light seemed to penetrate every corner, almost as if it cut through the rock in the walls, making the air glow golden.

One of the men was already up, sitting cross-legged on

the cot, with his eyes half shut and his hands joined in his lap as if in prayer. I watched his chest rise and fall slowly as he controlled his breathing. How long he had been at it I didn't know, but he kept it up for a long time before he finally opened his eyes and then walked out into the bright morning. I was surprised because I remembered the guard locking the door behind him when he left during the night.

Still feeling lazy, I lay and inspected the inside of the room from under the blankets. It was bare but clean. The walls were made of stone and the floor was covered with flagstones. Above the cot of the man who meditated, hanging from the roof on a string, was a contraption made of paper. It looked like a pinwheel and turned continuously in the breeze that swept through the room. The only difference between this building and the one I had been led to first was the absence of a stove.

In a short while the door opened again and the man who had been meditating re-entered. He looked strong and fit, but it was impossible to guess his age—he might have been forty or sixty. He went to his cot, sat down cross-legged again, and from somewhere produced a needle and thread, which he used to repair the seams of his shirt. The air was cold but he sat shirtless, sewing patiently. From somewhere outside a bell sounded and he tied the thread in a knot, bit it off, then put on his shirt.

The bell roused the other two men. They stretched and got out of their beds, carefully folded their blankets, then went outside. The meditator followed, but at the doorway he stopped and gestured for me to come with him.

The field was flooded in light. We crossed it at a quick trot and came to a canvas awning. Beneath it a man was stirring a pot that sat on a primitive stove made of stone.

The others had brought bowls with them and these were filled with rice gruel from the pot. An extra bowl sat on the edge of the stove. The cook filled this and held it toward me.

When we finished eating we rinsed the bowls, and then they were filled with a strong tea that warmed me. We breakfasted standing beneath the awning, except for the meditator who had taken up his familiar cross-legged position on the ground, just beyond the shadow thrown by the canvas.

After drinking the tea we rinsed the bowls again and started back toward the cabin. Before we reached it I heard a shouted command to come back, and turned around.

Behind the soldier who was calling to me I saw a table and chairs set up beneath another awning and the man I had spoken to the night before seated at the table.

That first time we said little. Mostly he questioned me about my case. He probably had received a report, but he wanted to hear my side of things. How much of what I said he believed, how much of the report, I don't know. We understood each other, though we had to repeat phrases often and sometimes make gestures with our hands.

We repeated the interview each day for five days. By then he had apparently learned what he needed to know about me and I did not see him for another week.

Life in the prison—for despite its informality that's what it was—was not intolerable. The food was Spartan but adequate, the blankets kept me warm at night, and the little work we were required to do—mostly moving stones to build walls or repair the buildings—was just enough to give us adequate exercise. Even after a week my body had not thoroughly adjusted to the altitude, and I frequently found myself dizzy and out of breath, but gradually this feeling lessened. No one could work really hard at that altitude. Even the men who lived there year round had to rest frequently if they attempted any physical labor, but in time I became comfortable and was able to do my share.

I'm not sure I believe in fate, but in this instance I think it had a hand in things. I could have been sent to any prison camp in Qinghai—there are thousands—and I could have met other commanders. Lobsang Lhalungpa was not like most. He was a man of moods—sometimes abrupt and brutal, other times patient and kind. There was a streak of the genius in him, a bit of the saint, and a lot of the devil. The latter was probably the saving element. It had enabled him to survive and climb through the ranks in an army run by Han who regarded him as an illiterate Tibetan savage and thwarted his ambition at every turn. I have no doubt that today he is still steadily, cunningly improving his lot. Put him down on the moon and he would do the same. In fact, Qinghai and the moon are not that different.

He came from a town called Jainca, in the eastern part of Qinghai, close to the borders of Gansu and Sichuan. His father was Tibetan, his mother Han, an unusual combination. The reverse is often true, for Han men stationed in Qinghai take native women for wives, but it is rare that a Han woman marries a Tibetan: To do so she must break with her family, a thing almost akin to death for most Han. But then Lobsang's father must have been an extraordinary man. He spoke of him seldom but when he did his words were respectful. His mother he spoke of continuously, with great love. He sent her most of his salary, which in Jainca probably enabled her to live like a queen.

His goal was to get as high as he could. "Privilege and

power—those are the only two things that one can work for in China," he told me. "If you seek wealth they will imprison you; women I have when I want them, but in truth they are cold-hearted—socialism drains the lust from their hearts and those who do still have desire live in terror of being criticized for their sins—but there is power. Power means better clothes, a warmer house, and good food. Power means servants and a villa near a lake for the summer months. Power means a red-flag limousine and a private room if one visits a big city and wants to eat in a restaurant. I will do what I must to get those things."

But he also had another side. Sometimes he chanted sutras and he liked to walk in the moonlight. He would travel fifty miles across the plateau, over rocky, almost impassable terrain, to find a lake where the fishing was good. He understood the Party and those who followed its strictures, but he also understood their weaknesses and saw clearly the stupidities they committed. He was hungry for success, but he slept until ten each morning. He could curry favor from his superiors, but he kept a list in his heart of those he would die for and those he would kill. When I encountered him he was in a fallow period. He had been the commander of the Zadoi Prison for almost two years. He wanted to move to a new place, to sleep with different women, to see new cities, but the leaders of the southern section of Qinghai were not cooperative. Perhaps he had made enemies; perhaps they thought a Tibetan should rise only so high. He was restive but he was not defeated. And somewhere in the back of a mind that Machiavelli would have been proud of, he was hatching plans.

"Canada is a powerful, rich country," he said to me one day during the third week I was in the camp. "You must have rich friends. Why do they not rescue you?"

"Because they are in the West and I am in China," I said. "Money is power only in a capitalist country."

He laughed. "Money is power everywhere," he said. Then he winked, and later that day envelopes, writing paper, and a pen and ink appeared on my cot as if by magic.

Later he stopped by the cabin to see if I had used them yet.

"Write letters to your friends," he said. "They will be worried about you. It is inconsiderate to let them worry. Write letters to your women and tell them you miss their warm beds and their soft bodies."

"How will these letters be mailed?" I asked. "The postage will be expensive—I have no money. The censors will read the letters. They will criticize you for allowing a spy to communicate with his countrymen."

He winked at me.

"Write letters," he said. "Let me worry about the postage and the censors. In China we close one eye."

"Did Mao say that?" I asked.

"A man far wiser than Mao," he answered. "But Mao learned from him—he was cunning enough to borrow from others those ideas which made his success possible."

"Such a man is wise," I said.

"Such a man becomes rich," he answered.

CHAPTER THIRTY-ONE

THE letters went out: five of them in all. I wrote to my brothers and three women that I knew. Two of them were wealthy—their own money, not their husbands'—so I had some hope on that score. The third had important connections; she was a doer of good deeds, an organizer of "save this" and "save that." She had a good heart, though. I was not optimistic; in fact I was cynical about the whole proposition. But what choice did I have? The Agency had written me off—that meant I did not exist as far as my own government was concerned. The only hope I had was the intervention of individuals. If money was the answer, and Lobsang seemed awfully sure of this, then it would do no harm to try.

Two days after I had completed and addressed the letters and they had been carried away by one of the soldiers, Lobsang had me summoned to his throne under the awning. He was in a jovial mood and before him sat a goblet filled with a brown-colored liquid. He pointed to a chair; I sat, and he pushed the goblet toward me.

"Taste this, Canadian!" he said. "If you like it I will have some brought for you."

It tasted like beer and licorice mixed together, and its

consistency was that of thin paste, but the kick was tremendous. My throat and stomach were on fire after a single swallow. I told him I wanted one too. He grinned, waved his hand to one of the soldiers, and in a few minutes another goblet sat before me, the aroma of the fermented liquid rising to my nostrils like smoke.

"This is a special drink for Tibetans," he said. "Made with herbs and the milk of the yak. It gives a man long life and potency."

He looked across the plateau toward great mountain peaks gleaming in the sun.

"Your women—are they the sort who give a man love, or are they like the Han women, cold and lifeless?"

"My women?" I said.

"There are three—to each you wrote fond words. You must be a strong man to have three women."

He winked and took a long swallow.

"Tell me," he said, "will these women help you? Are they rich women—the kind we read of in the newspapers?"

"Two of them are rich," I said.

"Ah, rich women!" he replied. "I knew a rich woman once, but she was old and ugly and smelled bad. Still, I would have married her but the gods would not have it so."

"The gods?"

"She died before the ceremony could be performed. My proposal had been accepted and the date set, but she did not live to see that glorious day."

"Bad luck," I said, and took a sip of the liquor. It had begun to taste better, but my mouth and throat were numb.

"Perhaps her family poisoned her," he said. "They were greedy and wanted her money. Two of her brothers were monks, one a man of great influence in the lamasery in Tingri. They did not wish a man of my humble birth in their family."

"Maybe the gods have something else in store for you," I said, for he looked truly sad now, like a child reminiscing about the loss of his first bicycle.

"The gods sometimes make things difficult," he replied. "Had they been kinder to me in this matter I would not be here but in Xining or perhaps Chengdu. With money a man can buy position."

"Great men must struggle against great adversity," I said. "The gods test their strength thus."

He looked at me with a cunning grin on his face.

"You try to humor me, my friend," he said. "We began by talking of your women and now we are talking of my poor life. That shows that I am truly a fool. The commander should direct the conversation, not the prisoner."

I took another sip of the liquor, knowing that I was as much in control as a cat playing with a lion.

"Tell me of your women," he said. "Is their skin as white as snow? Are their thighs soft and their breasts full? What words do they whisper to you, and who rides and who is ridden?"

I looked away and he laughed.

"The foreigner is as delicate as a woman," he said, and called for more liquor.

When it came his tone had changed; now he seemed more serious.

"Twenty years is a long time," he said. "Your crime is a serious one."

"My crime?" I said. "I was sentenced for telling the truth."

He tilted his head and looked at me through eyes squinted with suspicion; then his expression softened.

"In China there are many crimes," he said. "A man who does not understand the Chinese way can make grave mistakes."

Then I told him again of Liuyuan. During the first week I had told my story, but now I went into greater detail, describing the way people lived in the city and what they suffered. Before I had not told him of Xiyou, but now I did.

He listened to all of this sipping from his goblet and reflectively licking the corners of his mouth. When I had finished he pointed to my goblet.

"Drink! It will make the past easier to bear."

I raised the goblet and took a long, scalding swallow. When I set it down, a thousand stars seemed to be sparkling inside my head.

"The girl must have been beautiful," he said. "Was she?"

I said she looked like any other girl.

"Why, then, did you do what you did?" he asked. "All know that in China one does not say what the officials do not want to hear."

"I could not let the people in that town die," I said. "There was no other way to save them."

He shook his head. "Many die in China. No one can stop this. One can only protect himself and his family. No man is strong enough to save all the helpless ones; it is unrealistic. That is your real crime: you are an idealist. You should have studied Mao more closely. He has written much on this subject."

"We all have weaknesses," I answered. "Sometimes a man must do what is in his soul."

He laughed. "Perhaps in your country that is the way men live," he said. "But one cannot live like that in China.

Here that is the way of a dreamer. I have known many such men. Two of them sleep in the same cabin as you. They too committed the sin of idealism."

He looked away toward the mountains again; then he yawned.

"The day is sometimes too long," he said. "A man needs excitement, but there is little here."

"You should marry," I said.

"There are no rich women here, and I will marry only a rich woman. Perhaps you will take me to the West and introduce me to your women friends. Surely you can afford to give one of them to me. You do not seem like a selfish man."

We finished the liquor and he stood.

"Come with me," he said. "I have something to show you."

We walked to the edge of the camp, where a jeep was parked. He nodded to a soldier, who went into a cabin and returned with a key. We got into the jeep and Lobsang started it and backed up, grinding the gears as he did so; then we shot forward down the rough stone road that I had entered the prison on three weeks earlier.

The road led across the plain. We bounced from rock to rock; it seemed to me that we spent more time in the air than on the ground. Lobsang gunned the engine, oblivious to the beating the tires were taking. He drove on the road for three or four miles, then turned off on a trail that headed south, toward the distant mountains. A look of peaceful bliss had spread across his face, and he sang as he drove. He said the song was a Tibetan shepherd's song. It told of a young man's longing for his sweetheart. The young man spent long days and nights in the mountains herding his flock. He worried that his young bride would forget him and be unfaithful.

"Are Tibetan women unfaithful?" I asked.

Lobsang laughed.

"All women are unfaithful," he said. Then he commenced singing again.

We skirted a lake, its rippled surface as blue as a sapphire, then drove through a narrow valley with walls of a peculiar orange rock and emerged into a natural amphitheater, a flat space half a mile in diameter and circular in shape, surrounded on all sides by sheer cliffs sometimes rising as much as a thousand feet. On one side of this space there were a dozen dilapidated buildings. In front of one of them sat two shaggy dogs that stood as the jeep approached, their hair bristling and teeth bared.

Lobsang stopped the jeep in front of one of the buildings. The dogs took up a position ten yards from us, looking as if they would attack at any minute. The door of the building opened and a woman appeared. Her hair was plaited into two long braids that hung down her back to a place below her waist. Her smock, which the Tibetans call *champa,* was flowered, and she wore leather boots that reached almost to her knees. She had the same high cheekbones as the soldiers, and her skin was the color of copper.

Lobsang greeted her and she gave him a surly look; he gave her an ingratiating smile and said something and pointed to me. She looked at me curiously, then stepped toward the jeep so that she could inspect me at closer range. Her eyes filled with awe, almost as if I were a being from another planet. Lobsang laughed and said something else that annoyed her, for she turned and went to slap him.

They wrestled for a moment. She was strong, but he held her as if she were a helpless child, then pulled her to him and kissed her on the mouth. She tried to bite him, and let out a stream of obscenities, judging from their tone and her expression.

He spoke to her again, his tone soft and coaxing and his expression childlike. Finally she seemed to grow less angry, and he released her hands, turned her toward the doorway, and gave her a pat on the rump. She walked back toward the house, looking over her shoulder as she did so. Her eyes were still defiant, but her lips curled in a smile that revealed dazzling white teeth.

He stepped from the jeep, at the same time stooping and picking up a rock, which he flung at the dogs.

"Come with me," he said. "If you are to stay twenty years in Qinghai you must begin to live like the Tibetans."

The interior of the building was dark, and it took a few minutes for my eyes to adjust. I was aware of two other people in the room beside Lobsang and myself. I assumed they were both female but could tell nothing more. Then, gradually, I could see their faces. There was the girl Lobsang had been flirting with and two others. One was sitting so quiet and motionless on a rug in the far corner of the room that lay in deep shadow that I had not noticed her.

All three had copper skin and strong features. Their cheekbones were high, and each had a checkered scarf wound around her head. The one standing beside Lobsang's friend wore a purple *champa* edged with gold thread; the one sitting on the rug had a smock of a dark material, almost black, edged with bright crimson. She seemed the youngest of the three, but none of them could have been more than eighteen or nineteen; their skin was still smooth and fresh in a land where the skin turns to leather by the twenty-fifth year.

The girl in the corner began to play a sweet, haunting melody on a flute, and the others poured some liquid that tasted similar to that Lobsang had given me earlier.

Lobsang indicated that we should sit, and we did so. The floor was covered with rugs and a fire was burning in a small stove in the corner of the room. One of the girls opened the door of the stove and placed something in it, and the sweet smell of incense began to drift through the rooms. Then the two older girls seated themselves across from us, at a distance of about six or seven feet, and watched us drink.

The combination of the liquor and the incense and the music was powerful. The liquor was sweeter than that I had drunk earlier; it was strong but it did not make me dizzy or confused—instead a pleasant, euphoric feeling began to seep through me. Details became wonderfully clear. I felt happy and carefree, yet at the same time completely in control.

One of the girls rose and put more incense in the stove. The smell grew stronger—it was sweet, almost suffocatingly so, but the liquor seemed to float me above it.

The music had changed now and the tune the girl played on the flute was faster, almost teasing in its stop-and-go rhythm.

One of the girls stood and began to dance. She started slowly, moving a few steps, and then whirling round and round. She had removed her boots and danced barefoot. The music speeded up and she danced faster, her skirt fanning out. As she danced, she stared at Lobsang, her eyes fixed on him.

The other girl handed her a tambourine, and she banged it against her hip as she danced.

The music changed again; now it was slower, coaxing.

The girl sank to her knees and swayed from side to side with her head thrown back. She undid the scarf that bound her hair and threw it aside. Her eyes were still fixed on Lobsang, and now I could see the tip of her tongue, just visible, darting from side to side in her mouth.

The music speeded up and she leaped to her feet and began whirling madly, faster and faster, laughing as she became dizzy. I looked at Lobsang. His eyes were fixed on her, his gaze intent, but she returned it without flinching.

Again the music slowed. She fell to her knees and began swaying, first from side to side, then backward and forward in sinuous undulations. Then she leaned back until her shoulders were almost touching the ground and only her hips moved, rising and falling in an unmistakable movement. The music gradually picked up tempo again, and she moved her hips faster; then the music stopped completely.

Incense smoke drifted through the room. The only sound was the girl's heavy breathing. With a moan, she collapsed forward, reaching toward Lobsang as she did so.

He looked toward me and smiled.

"The other one is for you," he said. "Unless you want this one."

I shook my head.

The music began again and the second girl started to dance, her eyes fixed on mine. The music was as before, sometimes fast, sometimes slow and erotic. Halfway through her dance I realized that Lobsang and the first girl were no longer in the room, but I could not discover where they had gone, and I was certain the front door had never been opened.

This girl was slimmer than the first. Her teeth were like

snow and she laughed wickedly. When she collapsed onto her knees and leaned back and her hips began to move, as if they had a life of their own, I felt my pulse speed up. She moved faster and faster, then let out a long, agonizing moan that was half a shriek and collapsed as the first had done.

I found myself standing above the girl and reached for her, and her arms were around my neck and she was pulling me down to her. We rolled over and over. She laughed and bit me, staring into my eyes all the while; then she stood and removed her blouse and dress. Her body was lithe and strong, her skin shiny with oil. She pressed her hand between her thighs and slowly caressed herself. When I reached up for her she slid down to me with a low, throaty chuckle and sank her teeth into my neck, muttering "che-po" over and over again.

I awoke in darkness. Lobsang was standing above me, shaking my shoulder.

"Come, foreigner, we must return to the prison. We cannot stay here forever."

He looked at me curiously, laughed, and went out the door of the cabin. His look confused me, but after a minute I understood. I was lying under a shaggy blanket made of yak hide. On one side of me was the dancer, sleeping deeply, her mouth half open. On the other side lay the girl who had played the flute. She was much younger than the other—she could not have been more than fourteen or fifteen—and was curled up like a child. When I stirred she moaned and clutched my arm, and I realized that she was naked under the blanket.

I stood and dressed, shivering in the cold. Before I left I looked down at the two. They both slept soundly now, their faces peaceful, their breathing soft and regular.

Lobsang started the motor when I closed the door of the cabin. The sky was filled with stars, and his breath rose like steam in the cold night air.

"So now you have known Tibetan women," he said as we bounced along the road toward the narrow pass, our lights almost blindingly bright in the primeval blackness of the night. "Are they different from western women?"

I thought about the question for a moment.

"They are different," I said at last, "but it is hard to say how."

"Physically?" he asked, his eyes never leaving the road.

"No, not physically," I answered. "But their spirit is different."

He laughed.

"You are still a romantic! Spirit, bah!" He laughed again, the sound echoing into the silence of the Qinghai night.

We went often to the cabin in the rock amphitheater. That I wanted to sleep only with the slender woman he thought foolish—"Variety makes life interesting. The thin one is more flexible, but the other is stronger and more experienced." But I was finicky and insisted on keeping the same partner, and he agreed, though I had the feeling that sometimes he came alone, just to keep his hand in with the slim woman too.

The girl who played the pipe had delicate features and was hauntingly beautiful. When she spoke she cast her eyes down. She was not aggressive like the others but invariably would join one couple or the other in the darkness of the cabin, snuggling up to the lovers like a helpless child. Sometimes she sat and watched as I made love to the slim girl, her eyes devouring our movements, but the rest of her face demure and expressionless.

The days wore on and the summer began to die. Now the nights were colder and a stove was brought to the cabin where I slept. The other prisoners seemed to take this as a concession made to me because I was a foreigner, and they were pleased and nodded toward the stove and then pointed to me, then nodded back to the stove. The men spoke Chinese and we had exchanged words now and then, but they were close-mouthed and did not want to talk about themselves or why they had been sent to the prison. The meditator spoke only Tibetan. Sometimes he jabbered on for hour after hour, smiling, grimacing, gesturing with his hands, but I could only catch a word here or there. When I asked Lobsang about the men's crimes he said only, "They are idealists and they have met the fate of idealists."

I did not press him about this matter. About some things he was hard line. At times he could be a rogue ruled by nothing except whim and a desire for pleasure; at other moments, he was a model officer, the epitome of the Communist martinet. He switched between these different personalities quickly, without giving any signal. One minute he was smiling and talking about the hips of a girl he had once known, the next ordering a soldier to do his duty, his voice filled with iron.

He had great difficulty sleeping and often complained of this. "I have tried women," he said, "but it is awkward to have them here. If I have one then the others will want women. The men in the ministry who hate Lobsang and wish to see him reduced to a powerless sherpa would love just such an opportunity to criticize him. Still, I would chance it if I could trust the men under me, but I cannot. One never knows who will play the informer. Your best friend, a man you would have died for, will sell you out for the promise of a transfer to Beijing or Shanghai."

"It is the same in all systems," I said. "Men are treacherous—it is human nature."

"But in this system, my friend, it is worse. The evil comes from the strength. All men receive the same pay. An officer makes only a small amount more than a lowly foot soldier. It is thought that this is good because then none suffer poverty. But men cannot work for love alone; they are greedy creatures. You will never kill that instinct in them, not in a million years. And because our system does not give a man a chance to prosper by his merits, men seek other ways; they go through the back door. They slander their friends; they collect facts that will imprison a comrade; they make lists of men who speak against the teachings of the great Mao—" Here he raised his eyes in mockery. "I tell you men are greedy creatures and one way or another they must satisfy that greed."

He slapped me on the knee and stood. "Come—we talk too long of serious matters. The women are waiting for us and one should not keep women waiting—that is your western philosophy, is it not?"

We got in the jeep, and he backed it up, then spun the wheels as we turned and headed south.

"Is it true that in the West men are ruled by their women?" he asked. "I have heard it said that if a man would divorce a woman who has shamed him he must pay her a large sum of money. Is this true?"

I said the matter was not quite as simple as he had stated it; there were always two sides to any dispute.

He gave a snort of laughter.

"Such a custom is foolish. It would ruin all women."

I asked how that could be so.

"If a woman can shame her husband and be rewarded for the deed, all women will do so. Men will live in fear.

Their strength will drain from them, and their children will be sickly. Truly I cannot conceive how men can allow such a thing."

We had reached the canyon now, and as we entered it he beeped the horn long and loudly. The sound reverberated from wall to wall, growing in intensity until it was almost deafening.

"You are crazy," I said.

He laughed and threw his head back.

"We should let them know we are coming. That way they can prepare for us. Do you want to make love to a woman who has not washed the semen of another man from her body?"

I grimaced and he laughed.

"Ah, my delicate friend!" he said. "You want always to live in the world of the ideal. Facts disturb you, but the world is made of facts."

"You should write your own 'Little Red Book,' " I said. "You have more sayings than Mao."

"It is a good idea," he said, suddenly serious. "I will start tonight."

And after we drank and the women danced and we made love, he came to me in the darkness, jostling me out of sleep.

"Come," he said. "Tonight we cannot stay. I have to begin writing."

I groaned and followed him out into the cold night and listened as he muttered saying after saying on our drive back to the prison.

The first reply to one of my letters came early in August, almost two months after I had mailed them. The letter, from a woman I had lived with for a half-dozen years, voiced great concern for my plight. She said she would contact her congressman, even write a letter to the President. The very unsubtle suggestion that I had made regarding the value of money to grease the skids on the Oriental side of the divide was blithely ignored. Scratch one, I thought, and put the matter out of my mind. Lobsang did not understand.

"This woman cares for you," he said, "for has she not said she would write a letter to the American President himself?"

"It is nothing," I said. "In the West many men write directly to their leaders. Sometimes the messages are even answered. It is a custom."

He shook his head in disbelief. "No one would dare to do such a thing here—it would be considered an insult. Here if a man has a complaint he must speak to the leader of his unit, who then carries the message to another above him. The process continues until the message reaches the man at the proper level and a judgment is made. I wait now for almost a year concerning a request to move to Xining. Who knows but by this time next year I will still be waiting."

"Is there nothing you can do?" I asked.

He shook his head. "One does not hurry the authorities. They decide when they are ready. A man who complains only brings trouble upon himself."

The replies to my other letters arrived. My brothers also expressed great concern. One said he would personally visit his congressman; the other that his nine-year-old son had written a letter to the editor of a local newspaper telling of my imprisonment and that it had elicited comment. He wondered if this was good, however, for if my own government had disavowed me, then the letter might bring him under surveillance. He said he was sorry about the money but could spare none; and anyway he thought the idea had little merit, for if the Chinese had me in their power they could hardly be counted on to do anything but take any money offered them without doing anything to relieve my plight. "It's not like doing business with a western firm," he wrote, "for you would have no means of forcing them to comply with their half of the bargain."

When I read these letters to Lobsang, his faith in any immediate increase in his wealth began to wane, and when he talked of his future prospects his sentiments were grim. "A lifetime spent in Qinghai!" he moaned. "Such a life is empty indeed. Soon I will become old and drink myself to sleep every night. Me, who could have risen to great heights, who could have sat in a great office in Xining and spent my days signing government documents printed on fine white paper."

We had both almost given up when the last letter arrived, three weeks later than the first. It was from the doer of good deeds. She said she had discussed my case with a friend, a prominent lawyer, and that he knew of an organization that provided funds for such matters. She would need more details, however, and could promise nothing, but surely it would be worth the effort to try.

When I told Lobsang of the letter he smiled, clapped me on the shoulder, and immediately called for a drink. We were sitting under the awning. The air was pleasantly cool—the sunshine brilliant, a soft breeze blowing from the northwest. The liquor came, this time a great clay jug of it, and I drank until my head was spinning. All the time I wanted to caution him, to tell him that the money was not a fact yet, that its arrival depended on the reception of the letter I wrote in answer to the one I had just received, but I could not bring myself to dash his hopes.

Soon I found myself in the jeep beside him and we were bouncing along the road, heading for the rock amphitheater. He pounded the horn wildly in the canyon and leaped from the jeep when we arrived at the cabin.

The women were sleeping and stretched lazily and rubbed their eyes when we entered. Lobsang laughed and filled a goblet from the jug that he had brought with him and offered it to one of the women. It was the first time I had ever seen him do this, and the woman looked surprised and eyed him warily, as if he were addled. Then he got other goblets, filled them, and handed one to the other woman and another to the girl. They drank quickly and he filled the goblets again. Now they were a little drunk, and the liquor dribbled from their mouths as they drank.

Lobsang began to clap rhythmically and the women started to dance. They were unsteady on their feet but they whirled madly, laughing wildly as they did so. The girl had moved to the corner, where she picked up her flute and attempted to play on it, but she was too drunk and could manage only a few dissonant toots before she gave up and continued drinking from her goblet.

Lobsang leaped up and joined the dancers. He moved like a graceful bear, whirling round and round, clapping madly as he did so.

My head had stopped spinning, and I had begun to feel extraordinarily clear and detached. I watched as Lobsang and his woman crawled under a blanket on the far side of the room. The slim woman came to me and kissed me, but I did not want to make love, so she became angry and left to join Lobsang and his partner. I rose and walked outside.

Night was falling. I climbed into the jeep and watched the color slowly fade from the sky. The stars began to twinkle, first one or two, then a thousand. They were everywhere, filling the black velvet of the heavens with fine white powder.

Half an hour later Lobsang reappeared at the doorway, buttoning his shirt against the chill. He climbed into the driver's seat and started the engine without saying anything. Halfway to the prison he reached over and consolingly patted me on the knee.

"I am sorry," he said. "It was not my fault. Your woman came to me when I was drunk."

I told him it didn't matter, but he would not believe me.

"Now you will be angry with Lobsang," he said, "and you will tell your friend not to send her money to help you."

"It makes no difference," I said.

He muttered something that I couldn't understand, and then we bounced along in silence for several minutes.

"But I am the commander," he said suddenly. "And you are the prisoner. I will command you to ask for the moncy, and you will do as I say because I am the commander."

He was still drunk and he slurred his words a little.

"If you don't watch the road there will be no letter," I said, "for we will die in a crash."

He grabbed the wheel more firmly and stared ahead into the darkness.

"The skinny one is the better of the two," he said. "You have taught her well. Perhaps we should trade for a while so that you can teach the other one too."

"I won't be able to do that," I said, "for I must use my energy to prepare a letter for my friend. The letter must be perfect."

"Ah! The letter!" he said, his lips curling and his teeth flashing in a sudden smile. "Yes, it must be perfect. Think about it—think about it long and well, for it can mean much to both of us."

Chapter Thirty-Two

I TOOK infinite pain with the return letter I sent to my friend. In it I told of my imprisonment and how I had been abandoned by my government. I did not tell her I had been working for the Agency—the fact would probably not have gone over especially well with the liberal members of the charitable committee that considered such matters; but, even more, I was worried about the Chinese reaction if the letter were intercepted and read. Lobsang assured me that this would not happen—"There are ways; in China all things are possible!"

The letter went off, filled with vivid descriptions of my physical suffering and mental anguish and three repetitions of the fact that my sentence was twenty years. "With your aid," I wrote, "I can persuade the authorities to reconsider my case." It was double talk, but I knew she would understand, and so too would the people in the organization she had mentioned: they had dealt with such matters before, for my condition was not unique. The world was filled with poor fools who got in over their head.

Fall had come and with it the weather turned noticeably cooler. During the day the sun still warmed the air sufficiently so that men could walk about or work in relative comfort if they wore a coat, but the evenings were already below freezing and in the morning there was frost on the ground and the water in the well was covered with a thick layer of ice.

Lobsang seemed mellow. He was concerned about his potential windfall and each day asked if I had received an answer yet when I knew very well that he would know of a letter even before I would. But it was part of the game to give me the illusion that I had at least a modicum of power. Lobsang wanted me happy; he thought I would be more cooperative that way. A dissatisfied hen would lay no golden eggs.

Eventually the letter came. It was on a gray, overcast day—the first day when the sun had not shone since I had arrived at Zadoi Prison. I had been on a work detail all morning, stuffing the cracks between the stones in the walls of the soldiers' barracks with clay to cut down on the draft, and had returned to the cabin chilled, with numb, raw fingers. Until then, I had never heard the prisoners complain, for their treatment was benign, even gentle, but this day they were uncomfortable and they muttered curses under their breath.

I was the last in the door of the cabin, and I noticed that all three were staring at my cot. There sat a letter, resting like a misplaced egg. Perhaps word had spread concerning the importance of the letter, for the prison was small, not more than fifty men including prisoners and keepers, and a fellowship existed between the two groups so that gossip went back and forth readily.

The letter was typed neatly on the letterhead stationery of the organization my friend had mentioned. It was from the corresponding secretary of that organization, a name I recognized, for her husband was well known in international financial circles. The organization was the vehicle that allowed his wife to play the role of Lady Bountiful. They had considered my case, she said, but they were sorry that they could not help me. The reasons were gone into, the chief one being the strained relations between China and the United States owing to the dispute over Quemoy and Matsu. "The President's office has advised us that the sending of funds to the People's Republic of China is not advisable at this time," she wrote. "Should the political climate change, we will, of course, be happy to reconsider your case." The regal-sounding, hyphenated name appeared at the bottom of the letter. A distinguished-looking signature, I thought, and heartily wished her dead.

For two days after that I did not see Lobsang. My stock had fallen among the other prisoners, and I was no longer deferred to or given the best piece of yak steak or the first cup of tea. Word was about that I had proven a bust; it was as if the entire prison, both prisoners and keepers, felt its fate somehow linked with Lobsang's fortune.

On noon of the third day I was summoned to the table under the awning. The sky had cleared and the sunlight was so brilliant that I had to shade my eyes. A jug of liquor sat on the table, and Lobsang's goblet was half full. Apparently he was trying to drown his sorrow in his cups. He motioned that I should sit and I watched as he drained the goblet in a single swallow.

When he looked at me I saw infinite sorrow on his face, as if all his prospects in life had evaporated with my own chances for escape from Zadoi Prison. So pitiful did he look that I had to remind myself that I was the one condemned to twenty years in that place and not he. He drank off a second cup in silence, then took another goblet, filled it, and pushed it toward me.

"We are cousins in misery," he said. "It is a Tibetan custom. Men who share joy together must also share sorrow. Drink, foreigner! Drink!"

I did as he asked, for it was cold and I welcomed the warmth the liquor brought. He watched me as I swallowed, and I wondered what feelings lay behind that blank stare. If there were any true friendship between us this would be the ultimate test, for he had dearly wanted that money.

"Life is sometimes cruel, is it not?" he asked, more to the air than to me.

I nodded and held my goblet toward him, and he refilled it.

"When I was a young boy, hardly large enough to penetrate a woman," he said, "I often dreamed of going to Xining and living in one of the great houses that the officials live in. I had never seen these houses, but I had heard my father and uncle speak of how the people who lived in them did not have to draw water from a well or walk into the cold night to relieve themselves. I knew that such houses had electric lights that could be turned on at any time of the day or night. I had never even seen an electric light and imagined that it was a magical fire. I dreamed that I lived in a room where this fire covered the walls and the ceiling—that when I wished the walls to glow, they did so. When I told my playmates of my dreams they laughed at me and told me that I was a fool, someone who is sick in the mind"— he pointed to his head and made a circle with his finger—"but their jeers did not make me give up my plan. When I was ready to enter the world, my father died and with him all chance for schooling and easy advancement, for in those days before the Communist victory there was school only for those who could pay, and without my father we had little money. I worked at whatever job I could find—herding sheep, pushing carts, shoveling dung—no job was too lowly or too humiliating.

"I gave the small amount of money I made to my mother so that she did not have to wear clothes that were rags and eat food that was fit only for pigs. Many men asked her to marry but she would have none of them. She had loved only my father and she honored his memory. Finally a chance came for Tibetans to join the army and I was sent to Qayu—do you know Qayu?"

I shook my head.

"It is a place where none but Sherpas can live, high in the great mountains on the southern border of Xijang, which you foreigners call Tibet. There the air is so thin that men must rest after walking only a hundred meters. The camp was at the base of a great mountain and when the thunder roared, snow rushed down that mountain, great walls of snow that buried men forever. In the night it was so cold that men's fingers froze and their noses and ears turned black. We guarded the border because it was feared that the Indians would invade."

He refilled his goblet.

"Only Tibetans were sent to that camp, not even a Han to command us. Our leader was an old Sherpa who could not read or write. The Han paid him and he sent the money to his family, who would have starved without it. With each of us it was the same: we needed the pay, however little it was, and so we endured the misery. For months we did not see any other human beings. There were no women. Men made love to each other"—he made a face. "Truly it was a hard place. But I endured. In the cold nights when the wind blew and we waited for the snow from the great mountain to crush us, I thought of the great houses in Xining with electric lights. 'I will live in one of those houses one day,' I told myself, 'then all of this suffering will lie in the past.'

"Let me tell you a secret—I have never told this to anyone; no one knows, not even my mother. There is one thing I am more afraid of than anything else, more afraid of than any man or the snow that can bury a man or the cold that can freeze him. It is darkness. The blackness of the night. When I lie at night in my cot it is near a window so that I can see the stars and the moon. They alone give me courage, so here in Qinghai where the sky is almost always cloudless I am happy. But in Qayu it was not so: often great clouds hid the moon and the stars. The nights were blacker than death, as if the world had come to an end and everything had vanished. Each night I quivered with terror like a frightened maiden. One thing enabled me to endure—without it I would have become a lunatic, one of those who roam the countryside with a rag wrapped around them, begging for a few fen—and that was the thought of Xining and the houses with electric lights. 'You will have light,' I told myself, 'all the light you want.' And I would dream that I was in such a house and that when I wished for light the walls and ceiling would glow.

"I still fear the night, but now I have my own cabin and a lantern burns inside it all night. But a lantern is a poor thing—it is not like an electric light, which burns steadily and gives a beautiful white light."

When he finished speaking, he lay his head on his hands and slept. I sat on, thinking of his words and my hard fate.

Chapter Thirty-Three

A month passed; then, unexpectedly, a second letter arrived from the same friend who had written hopefully before. She said she was sorry that the organization she had first mentioned could not help and had contacted another, headed by a man who disagreed with President Eisenhower, a man so powerful that he did not have to concern himself with the President's wishes. She felt certain this man would help me. "You are just the kind of damn fool he has a soft spot for," she wrote, "so take heart. We'll scrape up the money somehow."

Because Lobsang had given up hope he had not bothered to have this letter intercepted and read, and I was afraid that the promise in it might turn out to be another bust, so I said nothing.

Several more weeks passed. October turned into November; now the days were cold and the wind blew unceasingly, so that when men crossed the space between the cabins they had to struggle to keep from being blown off their feet. The wind was everywhere, relentless, giving a man no chance to rest. It attacked him while he worked; it leaped at the windows of the cabin and managed, despite the hours we had spent caulking the stone walls, to penetrate the interior so that the men inside had to huddle around the stove. When a man went outside to relieve himself, he came back shivering; if he spit, the wind blew the sputum back into his face.

We worked less now, for only a few hours outside reddened our faces and turned our hands and feet numb. The wind howled at night and the air was filled with sand and pebbles. The prisoners wore scarfs wrapped around their necks and thick mittens of yak hide. Always the sky was perfectly clear and cloudless and the sunshine almost blindingly bright, which made the cold eerie; it was as if a man with a dazzling smile had suddenly drawn a knife and stabbed you with it.

I moved through the day mechanically, rising, eating, working, resting again, then sleeping. In the back of my mind was the knowledge that my friend in the States was working behind the scenes to secure the money that would help me. When the other prisoners cursed their fate, I worked silently, certain—although I had no reason to be so sure—that I would leave Zadoi Prison one day.

Lobsang and I continued to drink together, but now we drank in his cabin before the glowing stove. I no longer went with him to visit the women. One day I had stopped wanting to go, and after three or four rebuffs, he stopped asking me to accompany him. The thought that the person I was caressing would be caressed by another the next day or even on that very same day froze something in me and rendered the act a pointless mechanical exercise. Lobsang must have thought I was a fool, but he said nothing. He had pegged me an idealist, and the fact that my letters had so far borne no fruit served to show him, one more time, that idealists inevitably came to a sorry end.

Eventually a letter arrived from my friend telling me

that ten thousand dollars had been deposited in my name in the China Bank in Beijing. It could only be removed if I first contacted her, either by mail or phone, then signed off on a special form the bank would have. This bank had connections with provincial banks so that it would be possible to have the funds sent to a large town in Qinghai.

Lobsang and I had not spoken for several days. The last time, he had been more depressed than I had ever seen him. He could drink great quantities without showing any signs of drunkenness, but that time his eyes had been bloodshot and glassy and his speech badly slurred. He kept talking of the winter, when the clouds would hide the moon. "It will be black," he had said, "as black as the inside of a tomb." As he had spoken he had stared at the lantern, as if trying to draw some strength from its flickering yellow flame, which he might store against the coming darkness.

I wrapped a scarf around my neck, pulled on a Sherpa coat that the guards had given me, and went out into the cold. It was dusk and the sky was still pink, but a ferocious wind was scouring the rocky plain. I leaned into it and fought my way toward Lobsang's cabin. Every few steps I had to stop to catch my breath, for the wind was so strong and the air so icy that I could breathe only in quick, shallow gasps.

I banged on the door of the cabin but there was no answer, so I pushed it open and stepped in. Lobsang was asleep at the table, his head on his arms. An empty jug sat on the floor and an overturned goblet lay in front of him, its contents spread in a pool on the table. The flame of the lantern was leaping wildly in the draft, throwing strange, animated shadows on the walls. I tried to rouse him but he simply groaned and, after raising his head and blinking his eyes a few times, put it down again.

I took a seat opposite him, righted the goblet and refilled it, then took a long swallow. I was shivering because of the icy wind and needed something to drive out the chill. When I had drained the goblet I felt better and again tried to rouse him.

"Do not irritate me," he mumbled. "My head feels like it has been struck with a hammer. A man should be able to suffer in peace."

I chuckled and poured a small amount of liquor into the goblet and held it towards him. "The best cure for too much drink is some more," I said.

He shook his head but kept it cradled on his arms.

"I have good news," I said.

"What good news could you have?" he answered. "You are a man forsaken by his friends. You will remain in this accursed place for twenty years, and twenty years is a long time. We will grow old together as brothers."

"Ten thousand dollars," I said. "Twenty thousand yuan."

His head rose and he stared at me.

"You have not been forgotten!" he shouted. "One of your women has sent the money to save you!"

I nodded.

He threw his head back and laughed.

"Twenty thousand yuan!" he said. "Twenty thousand! With that amount I can move to Chengdu. Only fools live in Xining. I will move to Sichuan where the winds are soft. I will marry a rich woman who is also beautiful, not an ugly one. And I will live in a house with electric lights!"

Chapter Thirty-Four

I wrote a note to my friend, telling her to arrange for China Bank to send the ten thousand to a correspondent bank in Xining Lobsang suggested. We were almost four hundred miles away, but the towns in between were small ones. They probably had banks, but they would be manned by locals who would be confused by complicated transactions.

"We will travel across the plain together," he said. "I will show you the great and wonderful capital, then my home in Jainca. Doubtless Xining will not seem grand to you, for you have traveled much in the world, but to us it is a great city. The government offices are located there and the town is filled with cadres, riding in their cars with red flags and eating in their special rooms in the restaurants. And there are women—women who wear Western dresses and bathe every day and cover themselves with oil so that they smell like flowers."

We started early on the morning of a sunny day when the air was snapping cold. The rocks on the plain were covered with a skin of ice and our wheels spun as we bounced over the road that made a great snaking curve to the northeast. The sky was high and deep, a Qinghai sky that seemed to go on and on, merging somewhere with the infinite. To the north a single morning star glowed like a beacon.

Late in the morning we stopped and ate some pieces of flat bread and drank tea from a thermos; then we drove on. The sun was strong but in the open jeep the breeze was chilling, though Lobsang and the driver seemed comfortable enough; he slept, the driver smoked. I had buttoned the collar of my coat and wore heavy gloves, but my fingers still felt numb and I had not been able to feel my toes since half an hour after we had left Zadoi Prison.

Toward noon clouds appeared to the north, moving quickly westward, single file like a line of sheep. We still had not seen a living thing, either plant or animal. It was as if we were crossing the surface of the moon.

In midafternoon we stopped again so the driver could put up a canvas top, and drank more tea. By four the wind had begun to blow in earnest, sweeping down from the northeast. It slowed our progress and made the cabin of the jeep so cold the white plumes of our breath turned to crystal and fell as tiny flakes of snow.

At seven we stopped to eat some dried meat and drank more tea. Not more than a mile ahead, mountains began, and the road turned south briefly, then disappeared as it entered a steep-walled valley. The driver went to sleep, and Lobsang and I shared a cup of liquor from the great clay jug he had stowed among the drums of gasoline in the rear of the jeep; then he wrapped his coat around himself like a blanket and slept too.

I watched the mountain turn pink, then crimson, then gold as the sun set behind us. For a final moment the mountain flared up as if it were on fire; then, suddenly it was black and dead, a massive saw-toothed shadow that cut into the starlit sky.

★ ★ ★

The driver woke, started the engine, switched on the headlights, and the jeep lurched forward. Lobsang groaned but continued to sleep. I took a cigarette from the driver and smoked with the forlorn hope that it would warm me. The road skirted the bottom of the mountains; then we entered the valley and the sky was blotted out.

The floor of the valley was about fifty yards wide. Down the center splashed a stream. The road ran beside and sometimes cut across the stream, so that we had to cross and recross it. The water on the wheels turned to ice and they spun and we lurched, shot forward, skidded, then slowed, then shot forward again. Lobsang woke, cursed, and lit a cigarette.

"Not like your wonderful highways," he said. "This is an old road. It existed for hundreds of years before Liberation. Caravans going to Lhasa used it. The journey took months and sometimes, if there was a sudden storm, the river flooded, filling the valley with water. Men caught in here when that happened were drowned like rats and their bodies washed out into the desert, where their bones bleached."

The longer we drove the narrower the chasm became, so that at times it was hardly wide enough for the jeep to pass between the walls of rock. Now the water of the stream splashed under the wheels most of the time, sometimes foaming under the doors and wetting our feet. The driver and Lobsang smoked continually, and the air under the canvas roof became thick with tobacco smoke.

"We will reach the other end of the pass by dawn," Lobsang said. "There the road climbs through the mountains and there are no more passes until Bayan Har. You should sleep. When the flood comes it's so sudden that a man is helpless—it does no good to worry about it.

I gave him a rueful smile.

"We Tibetans are tough," he said. "Even today men sometimes travel this road on foot. The journey to Madoi takes them almost two weeks. They must carry all of their food, and the water is bad. If a storm comes, death is almost certain, but still men make the journey."

"What is there in Madoi that would drive men to take such chances?" I asked.

He shrugged. "A few thousand people. Women. Liquor. A hospital. Men who need these things are willing to make the trip. Not all survive but to those who do, it is worth the risk. Sherpas have always traveled in the mountains. We are not like the Han, who prefer to stay in their houses. We want to feel the wind on our faces and smell the clean mountain air. What is a man for if not these things?"

His eyes were fixed on something that lay ahead, in the darkness of the valley where we had not yet penetrated. There was nothing to be seen here, beyond the glow of the headlights, except blackness, but he was trying to peer into it, driven by the wonder of the unknown. Most Han would not understand that. The peoples were as different as water and fire. The Han lived together in villages and towns, in small, crowded houses. They filled their lives with rules and strictures, with infinite classes and categories that made a mockery of the "classless" Marxist society. For the certainty of shelter and food they would sell—had sold—their freedom. But men made a bargain only if they approved of the terms. For the Han the bargain had been a good one: freedom meant little to them; security and peace were their goals. Tibetans could not live like that; they would die—in fact thousands had already died—

if they were forced to live as the Han did. Lobsang was a man who walked a tightrope. He had cast his lot with the Han because he had no choice, but the life he craved—an apartment in a building in Xining and a desk in an office where he would sign papers hour after hour—would smother him. His life was a movement toward everything that was antithetical to his nature. I wondered how he would feel when he made that discovery. Would he flee back to the mountains, or live on, slowly drowning in paper and political meetings?

Suddenly the beams of the headlights no longer bounced back from the walls of the canyon but instead shot outward into the distance. The road began to descend gently and then we were past the mountains and on the plateau again. Far off to our right—we were heading northwest—the sky was touched with pink at the horizon. Dawn was breaking.

Xining was sprawling and dirty, surrounded by mountains. We came into it in midmorning, while the streets were filled with carts and trucks. Ugly buildings of gray stone filled the center of town, and the air was thick with smoke from factories.

"The bad smell is from a factory that processes dead camels," said Lobsang. "The meat is used for food, and the hide and hair are sold to foreigners who use them to make clothes."

We stopped in front of a rambling, faceless building, and the driver went in, then reappeared at the door and gestured that we should follow him. We were led to a room with three beds and lay down in our clothes and slept.

The sound of Lobsang and the driver's laughter woke me. They were passing the clay jug of liquor back and forth. The driver was talking and Lobsang listening with half his attention while he raised the jug to his mouth. Suddenly he broke into laughter at the man's joke.

He noticed that I was awake and held the jug toward me. I shook my head, and he shrugged and took another drink himself.

"We were discussing the merits of this city," he said when he had lowered the jug. "The driver knows many women and he was telling me of them. If you wish, we can visit them today."

I said that we should go to the bank first. He nodded.

"Business, foreigner. We should do the business first. You are right. Westerners understand such matters—that's why they are so rich."

I got out of bed and stretched, then walked to the window and watched the people passing. There was an endless stream of them, all dressed in blue, moving with the steady, calm gait of the people I had seen in Beijing. Only the children, who wore bright red scarfs of the Youth Brigade, smiled and laughed. There were many women pushing small wooden carts in which babies sat.

"Many children," said Lobsang. "Only five years ago Xining was a town filled with Mongols and Tibetans—for every Han there were three or four nonHan. Now the Han outnumber us. They come like locusts." He looked toward the driver and repeated the sentence in Tibetan, and the man nodded.

"Tibetans have many children but always some die. For every three born, one dies. Han children are hardier. The doctors are Han doctors and their medicine is good only for the Han. One day Qinghai will be a place of Hans."

He took another swallow from the jug. I pointed to my wrist, and the driver consulted his watch and held up three fingers.

"We must hurry," I said. "Soon the banks will close."

Lobsang lurched to his feet.

"The foreigner is right," he said. "Foreigners understand this world. Money is what makes it run, and now we will have money."

The bank was a small building on a side street. There were no other customers inside when we entered. Behind the counter sat a half-dozen people, some counting money, others entering figures in ledgers. We stood at the counter but no one looked up. After five minutes Lobsang roared, "Comrades!" and slapped his hands on the counter.

One of the clerks looked up, gave us a cold, appraising glance, then put his head down and continued writing in his ledger. Lobsang stared at him with eyes that would have bored a hole through granite, but the clerk worked on, as impervious to us as if we were thin air.

Finally Lobsang pounded on the counter and shouted, "Manager! Manager!" and the clerks looked up.

"This man is a foreigner," he said, pointing to me. "He is a rich foreigner and he has come to take his money from your bank."

One of the clerks rose and walked to the counter. He studied me for a minute, first my face, then my clothes which were the black, padded clothes worn by all prisoners. A look of contempt crossed his face and he laughed, said something to another clerk, and went back to his seat.

Again there was silence, broken only by the scratch of pens and the ripple of money being counted.

"He sees the prison uniform," I said to Lobsang, "and he does not believe that a prisoner can have money."

Lobsang nodded, frowned, then pounded the counter and yelled, "Manager! Manager!" again.

The irritated clerks raised their eyes; they couldn't count their money while he was yelling. Another man rose and came to us.

"The manager is not here, but even if he were he would not come—you cannot summon an official in that manner, you must show respect."

"Bah! Your respect smells like pig dung!" said Lobsang. "My friend is here to take his money from your accursed bank. If you refuse him service you will suffer for it."

The men eyed my prison garb.

"Do not be deceived by his appearance," said Lobsang. "He is a rich foreigner but he prefers to look like a poor Chinese prisoner. Westerners are strange."

The man looked at me out of the corner of his eye.

"Show him your name," Lobsang said, more for the man's benefit than mine.

The man slid a piece of paper and a pen toward me. I wrote my name and he studied it, then took it to another clerk. Soon an entire group had assembled. They looked at the scrap of paper as if it contained the signature of Mao Tse-tung. One of them went to a desk and removed a letter and carried it back to the group. They compared my signature with something written on the letter; then their voices rose in argument.

Lobsang looked at me and smiled. "You will get your money. Now they argue about details. None wants to be the one to release the money, but they know they must. They will try to cheat you, but I will not let them do that."

He pounded on the counter again.

"The foreigner cannot wait any longer!" he roared. "He

will complain to his leaders and all in this miserable bank will suffer! He wants his money now!"

The clerks exchanged glances, muttered a few words, now in a hushed tone, and one man was designated to approach us. He spoke to Lobsang without looking at me, his voice almost a whisper.

"The man says that they have never had a foreigner here before. For that reason they have been slow in granting your request. Now he is certain that they can fulfill your wish speedily."

He winked at me.

"You must hurry!" he said to the man in a half shout. "This foreigner is impatient. I will control his anger but cannot do so forever."

The man hurried away from the counter to a desk, where he opened a drawer, took out several stacks of bills, and began counting out my money. Lobsang stared at the growing stack of bills.

When the man had finished he went to another desk, took two forms from a drawer, and brought them over to the counter. He made an "X" on each, held a pen out to me, and pushed the forms toward me.

"The man wants you to sign," said Lobsang. I started to do this but he stopped me. "He is cheating you," he said. "First read what the forms say."

The Chinese characters were small and not clearly printed, and I had to struggle. After three readings I had discovered that the commission the bank would charge for handling the transaction was twenty percent. I told Lobsang and he shook his head.

"You are trying to cheat this foreigner!" he said loudly.

The clerk mumbled something, but Lobsang ignored him.

"This foreigner wants his money," he said again. "He is becoming angry."

He glared at the man and I did the same. The man wilted, backed away hurriedly, then went to the desk where he had gotten the forms, rummaged through a stack of papers, and hurried back to the counter with two more forms that he placed down and "X" 'd where he wanted me to sign.

I read the form carefully this time. It was simpler than the first: this time the commission was five percent. I started to sign, but Lobsang looked at me out of the corner of his eye and gave a little nod of his head that I interpreted to mean "no." Then he picked up the forms and made a great show of studying them.

"The American wants his money now!" he said, slamming them down. "He will not be cheated. He will speak to vice-minister Wang. He will criticize this bank and all who work in it."

The clerk grabbed the forms, scurried back to his desk, rummaged through the stack of papers again, then brought a new form to the counter. His forehead was beaded with sweat even though it was cold in the bank.

The form was the simplest of the three. The commission was one and a half percent. I started to sign and Lobsang placed his hand on mine.

"There has to be some record of the transaction," I said. "The commission is small."

There was suspicion in his eyes—probably he saw his fortune being stolen before he had even collected it—but I signed the form anyway and handed it to the clerk. He inspected the signature again, then went to his desk and compared it with that on the original letter. Again a crowd of clerks gathered around him.

Lobsang slammed his hands down on the counter and yelled, "Manager!" This time his voice was a roar.

The clerks turned and looked at us. There were more whispers; then the man who had given me the forms took the stack of bills he had counted out, added several more, and brought them to the counter and handed them to me.

I counted them carefully. There were 19,700 yuan in the stack. I nodded to Lobsang and we left the bank.

Once we were outside he broke into a great grin. "We must celebrate," he said. "We must buy some wine and celebrate."

We went to a store and bought four bottles of something that was as clear as water and tasted like two-week-old tea. Back in the hotel room, Lobsang and the driver drained two bottles before I finished my first glass. The money was still in my pocket. Lobsang had not mentioned it, but I knew where his thoughts lay. I took the money out, stripped off two hundred fifty yuan, then handed the rest to him.

He held it in his hands as if it were a precious jewel; then he started laughing. The laughter was deep and strong, bubbling out of him like water from an underground well. "I am rich," he said. "Rich . . . rich!" He kept repeating the word, as if he could not believe it himself.

CHAPTER THIRTY-FIVE

When I woke the next morning, Lobsang and the driver were snoring loudly. Empty bottles lay on the floor and the smell of alcohol filled the room. I went to the window and looked out. The alleyway was filled with bicycles, people peddling steadily on their way to work. Two policemen in white uniforms passed. Neither was carrying a gun. If I wanted to make a break for it, now was the time. With two hundred fifty yuan I could try to make my way to Beijing, traveling like a Chinese. The odds were long but anything would be better than rotting away in Zadoi Prison. And if they caught me, all they could do would be to bring me back. I had nothing to lose.

Asleep, Lobsang looked like a guileless Sherpa, a man who would play a wooden flute and climb with you to the top of a mountain. The truth was different. How far could I trust him? Would he simply take the money and forget his promise? It might even be convenient for him to kill me. That way he would be certain at least that I would not denounce him.

I slipped quietly off the bed and moved to the door, turned the knob, and opened it.

"It is too early to leave yet, foreigner."

The words came from behind me and were said in a clear, strong voice without the slightest touch of sleepiness in it.

"I was going outside to pass water," I said. "I cannot find the pot to use in the room."

"In the corner," he said, and I shut the door and turned.

He lay stretched out in bed, his eyes only half open.

"You do not trust me, my friend," he said. "And you would do something foolish. Such a thing makes me unhappy. Be patient. Now I must see some men and give them some money. Then the way will be simple. Do not be a fool."

I went back to the bed and lay down and tried to collect my thoughts. I could still wait for my chance and make a break for it later, but I would not get far in Qinghai, where a man could only move slowly. There was one train east, toward Xi'an. That was the train I would have to take, and they could check it. I might be able to hitch a ride on a truck, but they were all searched at the provincial border. Without Lobsang's help there was no hope. My fate lay in his hands.

I glanced toward him. He was watching me like a cat watches a mouse.

"The foreigner worries too much," he said. "He is too impatient. In China things work slowly."

Our eyes met and I saw something I had never seen before—a look that said "I have conquered you." I could have been mistaken—for what can a man tell for certain from another's eyes?—but I did not think so.

At ten we went to eat, and afterwards walked in the streets and smoked. Then Lobsang and the driver spoke in

Tibetan, and we turned down a narrow street lined with one-story houses of gray concrete with rusted metal roofs. The driver rapped on the door of a house, and a tired-looking Han woman with a hard face appeared. She quoted a price, and the driver looked at Lobsang, who shook his head. The driver offered a lower sum and she shook her head. This went on for several minutes. Finally an amount was agreed upon, the woman was paid, exactly half, and we entered the house.

The interior was dark except for a lone light bulb that hung by a cord from the ceiling. On one side of the room was a large sleeping platform covered with a straw mat.

The woman lay down on the platform and waited. Lobsang went first. The performance was over in five minutes; then the driver took his turn. When he had finished he stood, buttoned his trousers, and gestured to me.

I shook my head.

"The act is paid for," said Lobsang. "We have agreed on a price for three."

I shook my head again. The driver looked at Lobsang, who shrugged. The woman waited, her knees in the air.

"She is Han," said Lobsang. "It is difficult to buy such a woman. They are expensive."

I shook my head again. Lobsang indicated with a wave of his hand that I did not want the woman, and the driver unbuttoned his trousers and lay down on her again. Afterward, as we walked back to the hotel, no one spoke.

They slept through the afternoon and woke toward evening. Lobsang sent the driver for some food, and we ate in the room, then got into the jeep and drove south. Dust lay thick on the road, and it billowed behind us as we went.

The road passed through the center of a broad valley that angled to the southwest, between two large, barren mountains of yellow rock, then beside a dry riverbed. The sun was bright and the glare hurt my eyes, so I dozed. When I opened my eyes we were on a bridge crossing the riverbed. Beyond, the road entered a small town.

"This is Jainca," said Lobsang, "the town where I spent my youth. Tonight we will sleep in my mother's fine house."

It was the largest house in the town and was surrounded by a high wall of mud brick, painted white. The gate was open and through it I could see a courtyard filled with chickens.

The driver and I waited in the jeep while Lobsang entered. He walked to the house and called, but there was no answer; then he disappeared into a shed and a few minutes later reappeared carrying a pail of milk, called to us, and we left the jeep and stepped through the gate.

The milk was still warm. "From my mother's goats," he said, wiping his mouth on his sleeve. "She has the finest goats in Jainca. I brought them from the state farm in Xining. Such goats are rare."

The driver raised the pail and took a long swallow. Just then a short, stocky Chinese woman with strong features stepped through the gate. When she saw Lobsang she let out a shout of joy and rushed toward him.

They embraced and she stepped back and inspected him, then said something in Tibetan. She looked angry, and the driver laughed.

"She says that Lobsang has been sleeping with whores and drinking too much. She smells both the liquor and the women."

She spoke again. This time her words were sharper, and she pointed her finger at Lobsang.

"He has been commanded to bathe and to meditate," said the driver, struggling to control his laughter, for now the woman was eyeing him and her expression was the same. Then, as she looked at me, it suddenly changed and anger was replaced by curiosity.

Lobsang said something in Tibetan, and her eyes opened wide. She came closer to look at me.

"Take off your hat and let her see your strange-colored hair," Lobsang said.

She reached out and touched my head, then giggled like a schoolgirl and uttered some words in Tibetan.

"She says your hair feels like the wool of a sheep, not like the hair of a man," said Lobsang.

He said something else in Tibetan and pointed to his eyes. She moved closer until her nose was almost touching mine, peered into my eyes, and exclaimed excitedly.

"She says your eyes are the color of the sky. Such a thing she has never seen before."

We went into the house and sat at a table. Lobsang's mother put bowls of rice and pickled vegetables before us. All the while she kept staring at me.

When we had finished eating we went to a shed in which there was a large wooden tub and began filling it with buckets of boiling water. The air in the shed was cold and steam rose from the tub, as if it were a cauldron. When the tub was full we undressed and sank down into the water. I shut my eyes and leaned back and let the warmth seep into my pores. After about fifteen minutes Lobsang and the driver got out and dried themselves and dressed. I remained in the water, basking like a contented seal.

"Your skin will shrivel up like an old woman's," said Lobsang.

"I don't care," I said, without opening my eyes.

"Hot water weakens a man's member," he said. "After he has bathed he cannot please women. It is written so in the books of the ancient lamas."

"I don't care," I repeated.

They went out of the shed and left me alone. The water was still warm, and I was drowsy and fell into a half-sleep. For a moment I began to dream of the States and steak and whiskey, but the dream went nowhere. I could not let myself think of those things yet—they were too far away and there was still too much before me.

That evening, after we ate, we walked through Jainca. It was small and there was only one main street, crossed by a dozen alleyways. Lobsang pointed out the places where he had played as a boy.

"It is a poor town," he said, "but it was a good place to grow up. Then most of the people were Tibetan. We spoke our own language and played the games of Tibetans. There were monks and holy men and the city was filled with the smell of incense. Often we were hungry, but we did not complain. Tibetans are used to life being hard."

We stopped and he looked toward the riverbed, which was bone-dry.

"In the spring the river suddenly rises, foaming and splashing, so that sometimes there is water in the streets of the village, and we used to go wading. In the summer we would travel into the plain, herding sheep and goats and yak. Some of the men would move with the herds, always roaming. Men went away to the south, to the great city of Lhasa or to the monasteries of Trashi Lhumpo and Sera. Years later, they would return, traveling as the Tibetans have always traveled, on foot, carrying their food with them, their eyes still filled with the mists of the mountain passes and their skin burned brown by the sun. They would have tales to tell of the mountains, of passes like Mayum La, where they had walked among the clouds and heard the voices of the old ones. Children would gather round and listen as the men smoked pipes and told of nights when the wind spoke to them of places no man knows—of the land where the dead go. And those boys who listened would be infected by the stories, so that later, when they became men, they too would hear voices in the night telling them they must journey to the great mountains.

"But all of this was before the coming of the Han with their solders and their leaders. The Han brought us medicine; they built schools where we learn their language. They taught us to farm as they farm; they even built factories where we cure the hides of camels and yak. Once each did this work himself, selling the hides in the great market at Xining. Now the work is done in factories so that a man can cure as many hides in a single day as he once cured in a week."

I asked him if the work was as good.

"Not so good, but the Han want it so. They send the hides to Beijing and from there to foreign lands. It is said that there is great profit in these things.

"Now young Tibetans work in these factories. No longer do they roam in the mountains or travel to the south. To travel a man must have a paper signed by the authorities, and the authorities will not give such papers to Tibetans. They say that their journeys are wasteful, that they do not help the state."

He stopped speaking and looked off, across the dry riverbed to the plain. In the distance the snow-capped mountains had caught the last rays of the setting sun, and they suddenly loomed up distinct, great purple masses topped with crowns of gold.

"We have talked too long," he said. "It is time to return to the house of my mother and sleep. I must rest, for tomorrow there will be many things to do."

We turned and walked back through the town. Night was falling. Several bats suddenly appeared, as if by magic, fluttering in circles like giant, crazed moths, their high-pitched chirps filling the air. Lobsang stopped and followed their flight for a moment, his face filled with disgust.

"Rat-birds," he said. "They are as ugly as an afterbirth. Such creatures did not exist in Jainca when I was a boy." He paused, his expression suddenly grown hard. "They came later, soon after the Han arrived."

Chapter Thirty-Six

The next morning Lobsang and I walked to a house on the town's edge. When we entered we were greeted by an old man sitting cross-legged on a pillow. His face was cadaverous and his hooded eyes only half open. The man was dressed in the well-tailored suit of a cadre. He listened patiently to Lobsang, never once looking at me, then rose, went to a desk and took a piece of paper from one of the drawers, wrote something and put his seal on it. Lobsang handed the man a stack of bills. He counted them carefully, handed Lobsang the paper, and we left. When we were in the street again Lobsang gave the paper to me.

"This will give you passage to Beijing," he said. "From there you will have to make your own way."

I examined the paper. It was a single sheet, poorly printed. The seal on the bottom did not even look official, and it was smudged.

"And my sentence?" I asked. "How will you explain my absence to the authorities?"

"No one will ask," he said. "A man sentenced to Qinghai is forgotten. There are countless men like you. Those who share your cabin must remain in Zadoi till they die. They will speak to no one. And if, by some chance, the authorities ask about you, I will say that you died. Many die thus in Qinghai. It is a land of ghosts.

"A bus leaves for Xining at noon. It arrives in the capital at five. The train for Xi'an comes in at midnight."

"I will need money," I said. "Without money I cannot travel."

He eyed me coolly. "You have taken two hundred fifty yuan already. The ticket to Beijing is only thirty-five yuan. You will have enough money, my friend."

We were near the bus station now. The clock above the doorway said ten.

"I cannot travel in these clothes," I said. "They are the clothes of a prisoner."

"The paper says you have been released from prison," he replied. "Thus your clothes will not seem strange."

It seemed too simple.

"You have longed for this thing for months, and now when it is given to you, you are afraid," he said. "This is all I can do for you. The rest is for you to do. I have kept my word."

We gripped hands for a minute and our eyes met.

"Someday we may meet again," he said. "Lobsang will be rich then, and he will take you to the private room that the cadres use in the restaurant, and we will drink and eat and tell stories of the past."

The gray, ugly buildings of the city stood behind him. In the distance the mountains were glimmering in the midday sun.

"Take care," he said, then turned and walked off, moving briskly with his bearlike shuffle. At a corner he paused, waved, then turned onto a side street and vanished.

In the bus station I bought a ticket for Xining. The man who sold it to me eyed my clothes suspiciously but said nothing.

When I reached Xining I bought different clothes. My skin had been so burned by the Qinghai sun that it was no longer necessary to stain it. With a hat to cover my hair I could pass as a Uighur. In the paper I carried I was described only as a "Minzu"—a minority. The particular type was not considered important enough to be noted. From Xining I took the train east.

Very early in the morning we stopped in Xi'an. While the engine was being changed, a policeman boarded and stood just inside the vestibule, inspecting the passengers with cool, searching eyes. I hunched my chin down on my chest and tilted the cap forward so that the visor shaded my face. I could feel myself sweating.

The minutes stretched out. The conductors were washing the windows of the car; steam rose from the hot water in their buckets. The policeman was studying me; I kept my gaze fixed on the conductor and the platform outside. If the man was thorough he would question me and ask to see my papers.

The whistle blew and the conductors poured the water out of their buckets and reboarded the train. The doors were shut and we began to move again. I breathed a sigh of relief and shut my eyes. I was almost asleep when I felt a hand on my shoulder.

The policeman looked at the paper; then he peered at my face and asked what I intended to do when I reached Beijing.

"I will recontact my unit," I said.

He glared at me and I looked away. Look frightened, I thought, a released convict should be afraid.

"What is your unit, comrade?" he asked.

"The Ministry of Culture," I said.
"Your job before re-education?"
"A clerk," I answered. "I worked in the Minzu Exhibition Hall."
"Your crime?"
"I struck a foreigner," I answered.

He gave me one last long look, then handed the paper back to me and returned to his post by the exit.

I looked out the window and tried to control my breathing. None of the other adult passengers were looking at me, only the children. The adults were too cowed. Each had listened to the questions—they could probably have repeated them verbatim—but they were too intimidated to yield to curiosity.

Toward the end of the afternoon the land flattened out into a dull, monotonous plain. The roads were straight as a string, and truck after truck rolled down them, all heading to the northeast toward Beijing.

We reached the outskirts of the city at ten, and half an hour later I walked out of the station into the cold Beijing night.

Chapter Thirty-Seven

The Canadian embassy official stared at me in disbelief. "You were imprisoned for traveling without a passport and for slandering the Chinese government?"

I nodded.

"Your name?" he said, a skeptical expression on his face.

I told him, but there was no reaction.

Then he asked if I remembered my passport number. I could have said "no" but that would only have slowed them down. In the end it would have amounted to the same thing. So I gave him the special Agency number. He took it down, then made a phone call and gave someone in another office the number.

I sat for five minutes while he stared out the window and fumbled with his pencil. He was so closely shaven that the skin on his face was raw and painful-looking, and there was something stiff in his expression and manner, effeminate yet unyielding the way men afraid of their effeminacy sometimes are.

The phone rang and he picked it up, and I watched his expression change: first alarm, then shock, then an attempt to look composed.

"There is some problem," he said, the hesitation in his voice giving him away. "The office will require some time to investigate the matter."

"If the security police pick me up they'll put me back in prison," I said. Then I smiled and added, "If you can't come up with something better, I'll have to tell my story to the foreign journalists. That way I'll be sure that if they do get me, the world will know about it."

His hand started to shake and beads of perspiration formed on his forehead. I could imagine his thoughts—a career down the drain; lifetime assignment to a place like Dacca or Ulan Bator.

"You're liable to have a real mess on your hands," I said. "Your brothers to the south can become pretty nasty if one of you guys fouls up."

He picked up the phone and made another call. This time he spelled things out clearly. I had underestimated him: motivated by fear, he was actually a bit tigerish. When he hung up he looked calmer.

"We'll issue you another passport. It's irregular but it can be done. You'll have to wait half an hour."

"I'm short on cash," I said.

"We can help you," he replied, with a smile that was all teeth.

"Can't beat the good ol' US of A and Canada for efficiency," I said.

He laughed awkwardly.

"Where are you from?" I asked.

"I was in Ottawa for the last five years," he said. "Before that I was stationed in Washington."

"Ever know a stupid son of a bitch called Hildebrand?" I asked.

They worked it out just about as I had expected them to. You can count on their logic. Whatever was best for the Agency: always the larger consideration. I was free now, in limbo but free. They weren't worried about my leaking information because they assumed that if I were going to do that, I would have done it already, but they were afraid of the press. A story about a spy hurt everybody. If I went to the Western journalists and told them that I had been abandoned by the Agency, the stories they concocted could rock the organization to the foundation. Directors had been asked to submit their resignation for less.

So I got a new passport with a new name: Richard Alston. I asked for my original name, but they thought that was unwise. "Why cause a ruckus?" said the fat man who issued me the passport. "The security police may be looking for you under that name."

I shook my head. "They think I'm still in Qinghai," I said.

"We can't count on that," he answered, and handed me the passport. I inspected the picture on it that they had taken half an hour earlier. The man in that picture looked worn. There were lines around his eyes and his stubble-covered cheeks were hollow. He looked like a refugee. He might have been from anyplace where the living was hard. The face betrayed no emotion; it belonged to no identifiable nationality.

The sky was gray when I left the embassy. The PLA soldier guarding the gate gave me a wary look. He wasn't sure about me. My face was Western but my clothes were Chinese. He probably wondered if he had made a mistake in allowing me to pass. If so, the best thing to do was to pretend that nothing had happened.

That afternoon I checked into the Peking Hotel, took a

bath, and ate a big lunch, then went to the Ministry of Transportation. It was the hard way, but I didn't know any other way to start. In China there are always records. Xiyou had worked for them, and if anyone knew where she was, they would.

The woman listened to me patiently. There was a look on her face that said it was impossible. She knew, but she was too polite to tell me straight out.

"I must find her," I said, knowing that as long as I could talk with the woman there was a chance. If she felt my motives were good, she might help me.

"Her uncle lives in Canada," I said. "He has not seen her for almost ten years. He asked me to visit her. The uncle worries about her night and day; I must see her with my own eyes so that I can tell him that she is well. The uncle is too old to worry; he should live out his days in peace."

Her expression clouded and I knew I had taken the wrong tack.

"If she is not well," I said, "I will not tell him. Instead I will say only that I saw her. If he asks about her health I will tell him that she is resting. I would not want him to worry."

The expression in her eyes had turned kindly again.

"It is hard when families are separated—it is sad for the old people when they cannot see their nieces and nephews," I said.

She was not persuaded yet, but I was getting there.

"When she was very young the uncle made a promise. He said that even if they were separated by a great distance—even if they were on other sides of the world—if she was sick and suffering he would help. Such promises are sacred."

She gave me a searching look, then went to a bank of drawers that covered an entire wall from floor to ceiling and began to hunt for a special drawer. She found it in the top row; to reach it she had to climb a ladder.

She brought the folder back to the front desk where I was standing and studied the documents in it carefully. There were several official-looking papers with seals affixed at the bottom. She read these, then closed the folder.

"She is in Beijing," she said, and I felt my heart speed up; then I noticed something in her eyes.

"She is not well," I said.

She nodded. "She is in a hospital on the northwest edge of the city. I will write the address and you can give it to the taxi driver."

Chapter Thirty-Eight

The taxi passed houses and compounds with chickens pecking in the courtyards, then turned off the main road and took a twisting, dusty dirt road through dead winter fields. We went through a gate and a man in a guard house waved us on, then went back to sleep. There was a brick wall about twenty feet high surrounding the building; a fence of barbed wire sat atop the wall.

Just inside the front door a man sat behind a desk, reading a newspaper. I expected him to be surprised when I entered, but he wasn't: he had a face that looked as if nothing could ever surprise him. I handed him the letter the woman in the Ministry of Transportation had given me, and he rose and left the room. Fifteen minutes passed; then he returned with a middle-aged woman who had a sour face and a hard, brusque manner.

She motioned that I should follow her and led me down a long hallway lined with doors. Each had a window covered with bars. At the end of the hall we came to some steps and climbed to the second floor and passed through a set of swinging doors. Here there was another man behind a desk, with the same blasted look as the man at the entrance.

We entered a great dormitory, filled with bed after bed. People wandered back and forth aimlessly. Some sat in groups playing cards; some were staring into space. At both ends of the hall sat female attendants in white. The woman guiding me approached one and showed her the letter.

They took me through the dormitory and down another long hallway. Halfway down it they stopped at a door, and the attendant took out a key ring. The fifth key she tried worked and the door swung open.

The room was bare, a pallet in one corner, no chair or table. Xiyou was sitting on the floor staring out the window. There was a grate of thick screen over it and the glass was dirty, but it let her see a little of the fields outside.

She didn't turn when we entered. The attendants waited, as if they expected me to do something, but I could not bring myself to call her name. Finally one of the women approached her and put her hand on her shoulder, and she twisted her head and looked up.

Her face was the same—an ordinary Chinese face, not ugly, not pretty, the eyes expressionless. For a second there was a glimmer of something, but whatever it was went out.

I asked the women to leave us alone, and they left the room, leaving the door open behind them. One returned in a moment with a chair and sat where she could watch us.

I sat on the floor beside Xiyou. She had resumed looking out the window. "I wanted to return to Liuyuan but I could not," I said.

Again there was a flicker of something; I could not see it but I could feel it—as if somewhere in the ice of her soul a fissure had opened.

"I tried to tell the leaders in Hami about Liuyuan, but they would not listen. They said that my words slandered the state, and they sent me to Qinghai."

"The leaders are good," she said in a flat voice that sounded like one of those recordings you get when you reach a disconnected number. "The leaders want to help the people."

Then she was silent again.

"You must get well and leave this place," I said. "Your friends miss you. Your mother and father mourn you."

"The leaders have assigned me here," she replied. "When the leaders tell me to leave I will leave. The leaders are good. I trust the leaders."

Her eyes told me something different from her words, but that part of her was buried within, behind walls that I could never knock down.

For almost an hour I sat beside her in silence and stared out the window. It was midday but the sky never brightened. When I stood to leave, something flickered in her again. She looked at me and in her eyes was all the hopelessness that lay within. Those eyes knew about the desert she lived in, and though they had never known anything but that desert, they knew that somewhere in the world there was sunlight and laughter. That part would not die—nothing could kill it—but all the rest of her, everything she had been taught and seen, wanted it dead. She had made a truce between that part and the rest. The conditions of that treaty were simple: she would stay in her cell and peer out the window until the leaders she believed in saved her. It would be a very long time.

The trip back to the hotel seemed to take forever. It was only midafternoon, but the streets were clogged with slow-moving traffic. The taxi stopped at an intersection, and I watched the flood of people cross the street. It was a gloomy day, and the people's blue caps and trousers looked darker and more sombre than usual. They moved in an orderly chaos: none hurried, none lagged.

When I got back to the hotel I went to my room and lay down. It was all over. I had kept the promise I had made; the thing that had driven me for months could not drive me any longer. There was one more thing to do, and I wanted to do it as soon as possible. Then I could go.

Chapter Thirty-Nine

The cab rode up the inclined drive to the entrance to the Friendship Hotel. I climbed out and went into a lobby filled with people. A dozen Hong Kong businessmen stood in the center. On one side of the lobby there was a desk where money was changed. There was a crowd around it. Opposite was an information desk; at the front of this was a felt-covered board. Mail that had never been claimed was placed here. Much of it was nearly a year old. I could see the package I had mailed from Hami on the upper right-hand corner of the board. An attractive young woman behind the desk was reading a book. If I approached and took the parcel she might ask for identification. She probably wouldn't, but I didn't want to take the chance.

I ambled over to the businessmen and asked them how long they had been in Beijing.

"Three days," said one.

"That's three days too long for me," said another. "This is a boring town."

There was a chorus of nods.

"Have you been to the Minzu Palace yet?" I asked.

They shook their heads.

"That's where the girls are," I said.

"Girls?" said the man who had spoken first.

I nodded.

"Where is this Minzu Palace?" said another, who had a cigarette dangling from the corner of his mouth.

"Ask the woman at the desk," I said, gesturing toward her. "She'll tell you."

They went to the information desk and spoke to the woman. While she took out a map, I slid around to the front of the desk and took my parcel.

As my cab glided through the empty streets of the city I opened the letter. The papers were just as I had mailed them. Tomorrow I would send them out through the diplomatic pouch at the Canadian embassy and book a flight. If I was lucky there would be a cancellation and I would be out of Beijing by nightfall.

At two the next day I left the Peking Hotel. The drive to the airport took forty-five minutes. The road was empty of traffic except for a few trucks; near the airport it was lined with trees like the roads in France.

The airport wasn't crowded, but I had a long wait for my flight. I thought that when I finally boarded the plane I would feel a flood of relief, but it wasn't that way. I just felt very tired and empty.

The plane taxied down the runway, lifted off, banked to the east, then climbed. Below, China slipped away to the west, back into the past. I shut my eyes, and when I woke again we were far out over the Pacific.

If you have enjoyed this book and would like to receive details of other Walker mystery titles, please write to:

    Mystery Editor
    Walker and Company
    720 Fifth Avenue
    New York, NY 10019